For my father, Kenneth.

First published in the UK in 2019 by Nosy Crow Ltd
The Crow's Nest, 14 Baden Place
Crosby Row, London, SE1 1YW, UK

www.nosycrow.com

ISBN: 978 1 78800 360 5

Nosy Crow and associated logos are trademarks and/or registered
trademarks of Nosy Crow Ltd

Text copyright © Ellen Renner, 2019
Cover and inside illustration copyright © Jedit, 2019

The right of Ellen Renner to be identified as the author of this work
has been asserted.

A CIP catalogue record for this book is available from the
British Library.

Printed and bound in Great Britain by Clays Ltd, Elcograf S.p.A.
Typeset by Tiger Media

Papers used by Nosy Crow are made from wood grown in sustainable forests

1 3 5 7 9 10 8 6 4 2

I

The enormous shadow of a seabird slid across the waves and fell upon the *Wayfinder*. Storm, sitting in the stern of the ship, felt the hairs on the back of her neck stir.

She slipped her tablet and drawing stick into the leather pouch at her waist and waited for the threat to make itself known. Lake, captain of the *Wayfinder*, stood a few paces from her, bare feet gripping the deck, hand light on the tiller. He was humming under his breath, his thickset body swaying to the sea's dance. It was obvious that her uncle hadn't seen the Air spirit's warning. She was used to that – the Albatross seldom appeared to others.

Storm was a witch: last year, when she had turned thirteen, the Elemental spirits had given her power over both Air and Water. Now she stood up and began to look for any threat lurking in the watery hills of the Second Sea. Storm counted eleven ships riding the waves in diamond formation behind them – all that was left of Yanlin's once mighty fleet.

The enormous white and grey wingspan of the Albatross suddenly appeared, tracking its shadow, circling over the following ships like the bird of prey it was. Storm's stomach began to squirm the way it did whenever she saw any of the Elemental spirits. There was no sign of the Dolphin, but the Water spirit was seldom to be counted upon.

"Hey, Storm! You spotted something?"

It was Cloud, a childhood friend who had sailed with the fleet the previous year, the year of the Drowned Ones' attack on Yanlin Island. Cloud had been lucky: he had survived. Many had not.

"Back to work, boy!" Uncle Lake's larger-than-average nose turned at once in their direction; his nickname with the crew, she knew, was "Trouble-sniffer". "You're supposed to be in the galley, gutting fish."

"I've finished, Master. Can I climb up to the crow's nest and spell the lookout?"

"How many times do I have to tell you that junior

apprentices don't do lookout duty? If there aren't any fish to gut then go and mend nets!"

Cloud's eyes flashed rebelliously, but he retreated below deck.

Storm's uncle sighed and turned to her. "Do enemies threaten?"

"I don't know. Maybe." She swayed to the roll of the boat that was part of her now, like breathing. The fleet had left Yanlin harbour only three five-days ago, yet it felt like she had always lived aboard this ship. She had become two people – the new seafaring Storm and the barely remembered girl who had died along with her mother.

At Lake's words, every pair of eyes on deck fixed on her. Storm felt her face grow hot. She was aware of the crew's growing belief in her power and wished she could share their confidence. All because the Elementals had chosen to make her a witch! She would never get used to it – never lose the fear of failing these men, as she had failed Dain.

She pushed the memory of her mother from her mind and glanced again at the Albatross, high overhead. *What is it?* she asked, knowing her plea was useless. The Elementals communicated only when they chose.

But this time the Albatross replied: it sent mist to

thicken the air, and Storm's stomach turned over. "Enemies near!" she cried.

Lake shouted an order, and the lookout high in the nest on the main mast sounded the warning bell. Its iron voice clanged across the waves. The other ships were fading ghosts in the thickening fog, but Storm heard their bells answering.

And then, beside them, out of the belly of the sea, rose the dark shape of the Dolphin. The Elemental shot into the air, larger than the ship itself. Storm flinched as the spirit rose silently from the sea, blotting out the last of the light. The Dolphin cleared the *Wayfinder*'s three masts and slipped, sleek and dangerous, back into its Element.

"Lower the boat!" Storm shouted to Lake, shuddering away her childish fear of the Water spirit. The Albatross and Dolphin had both shown themselves in warning. The threat was severe. She must seek out the enemy before they could attack.

Her uncle obeyed her without question: thrice now she had sailed alone to face an enemy; thrice she had conjured a gale and blown predatory ships from other islands into the far distance. In a heartbeat, a small rowing boat was in the water. Storm ran to the rope ladder held by two sailors. She was startled to see that one of them was Cloud. He would get in trouble for sure this time.

"Good luck! Wish I could come with you." Cloud thumped her shoulder in encouragement.

Storm nodded and swung herself over the side, barely noticing the longing in her friend's face. She clambered down the ladder and dropped into the plunging boat. The mist closed around her as she took the oars and rowed deeper into the fog. Once clear of the ship, she shipped the oars and let the Dolphin take the boat where it would. This was hardest of all – allowing the Elementals complete control.

She could see nothing but thick, grey-white mist. It was cold and damp, soaking through her clothes and into her hair. Water began to drip off the end of her nose. Storm sat, heart thudding, fingers clenched around the oar shafts, listening to the slap of the waves against the hull. The boat moved steadily through the water, as if pulled by a rope. She closed her eyes and waited.

Her boat slid to a stop and magically floated in one spot as wave after wave passed beneath it. Storm's heart pounded harder; she readied herself. The Albatross's wind whistled towards them from the direction she knew instinctively was north. It blew away the mist.

Fear and hatred squeezed the breath from her lungs as Storm saw that the predator closing in on Yanlin's fleet was an enormous raft town! The Drowned Ones rode the waves only a few oar lengths away. The tribe of landless sea-dwellers had attacked Yanlin last year. Crews of ships captured by these sea pirates faced death, not mere robbery.

But surely it wasn't the same raft town she had defeated in Yanlin Harbour. Because that would mean…

In that moment of doubt and disbelief, Storm saw her enemy. One face, among dozens. He, of all of them, was looking in the right place. Their eyes met, and Storm saw Nim, the Drowned One boy, turn the colour of ash.

Later, when she strove to record the attack in the drawings she had begun to make as a sort of journal, she could hardly order the events in her mind.

She remembered hate swelling her skin until she thought she must split in two. She jumped to her feet, readying her magic – the music of the Air. She would call the wind and punish those who had murdered her mother!

Nim shouted. His mouth was a circle of fear; his eyes fixed on her. Later, she thought she remembered hearing him calling her name, as if in warning. But that was impossible – she knew the worth of the Drowned One boy. She had trusted him once and betrayal had been her reward.

It was in that moment that disaster struck. Storm's head flooded with memories of her dead mother – images and thoughts she had tried to bury with Dain. She struggled to focus. She searched for Air-music, but all she could hear was a white buzz of loathing. Storm looked into the eyes of the boy who had caused her mother's death and knew she was about to die.

Nim's cry had warned them. He looked horrified, orange freckles stark in a sweaty face. Twenty-four arrows were notched, aimed, loosed. The shafts rose into the air as one, like a flock of startled birds. Storm thought of her mother. She would see Dain soon.

Not if your body is lost, fool! shouted her mind-voice.

The fear of final separation broke the spell. Storm dived into the sea a gasping mini-breath before the first arrows thudded into the wood of the rowing boat, turning it into a floating porcupine.

A finger of pain scratched her shoulder, the salt-burn of seawater on raw flesh. She was shot! Terror dissolved the feelings of unreality. Storm flailed at the water, fighting it, her ears full of the enemy's shouts. Sea-splashed eyes glimpsed bows drawn taut, arrows bristling, as she filled her lungs and ducked underwater to take refuge beneath the boat.

She was in the Dolphin's kingdom, but the Elemental seemed to have abandoned her. Disgusted, no doubt, at her ineptitude. A muffled drumming bubbled in her ears as a second shower of arrows plunged into the water around the boat. She watched the shafts wobble as they met the Element's resistance, slow, turn to float to the surface. The third downpour came, and an arrow grazed her leg. Storm's lungs began to burn hotter than her shoulder. All day long, she had seen sharks hunting these waters. Her blood would bring them. She must do something! The Dolphin and Albatross would not save her if she did not even try to save herself.

Storm made her body relax until she floated beneath the rowing boat as if already dead, head back, arms and legs drifting. The pressure in her lungs eased, and she found she could hear the music of Water at last – an endless surging, a flow-and-ebb, like the heartbeat of a leviathan. And through the beat came a wriggling-jumping-trickling thread of power. Her mind grabbed the thread and she felt its power flow into her. When Storm was shining-full of the Dolphin's power, she focused a single thought and willed the magic to its work.

The sea rushed away from her, rose in a wall of water, higher and higher. She was sucked behind, dragged in the wake of the mountainous wave surging towards the raft town of the Drowned Ones. She bumped and spun along the seabed. At last her body rose to the surface. Swallowing as much water as air, bruised and battered, Storm was tossed from wave to wave like a piece of limp seaweed. She found a leftover fragment of power to calm and thicken the water beneath her into a moss-wet mattress.

She sprawled on her stomach, coughing and spewing. The wind brought the sound of swearing and screaming growing ever fainter. The raft was still afloat! The wave hadn't crushed the pirate town, it was merely driving the enemy before it.

"No!" Storm screamed at the sea, at the Dolphin's betrayal. She listened, frantic, for a hint of Water-music, but all she heard was the slosh of the sea and seagulls crying overhead as they circled, hoping to make a meal of her eyes if she died. She had lost her magic again. She had failed Dain, failed Thorn. The enemy lived.

2

"You should have sent a second wave to sink the raft! You had a chance to kill them! Why didn't you finish it?" Cloud paced back and forth, hammering his fist into his palm, over and over.

"Don't go on about it!" Storm lay in one of the below-deck hammocks, staring at the ceiling. She wished Cloud would go away: he was making her head hurt.

The Healer had cleaned and bandaged her shoulder and leg. She had lost enough blood to feel light-headed, but she longed to be above decks. She couldn't think, shut up down here. And she needed to think. Why had her Water-magic failed after that first attack? Was it her or the Dolphin?

"I tried," she muttered. "I couldn't manage it. Sorry."

"You couldn't have really tried. A *proper* Weather-witch would have finished the job! I would have, if I was a witch. Maybe you just aren't brave enough."

"What does that mean?" Storm pushed herself up on to her elbows.

Cloud had stopped pacing to glare at her. "This isn't the first time you've failed us! You let two of the raft towns escape after the attack on Yanlin. And now they come to finish their job because you didn't have the courage to kill when you could! Have you forgotten Thorn?"

Storm swung out of bed and nearly fell as her legs gave way. She grabbed the hammock with both hands and stared at him. "Have you forgotten that my mother died in their raid?"

His face flushed red. "Sorry," muttered Cloud. "I … I didn't mean it." His voice was strangled with frustration – he still doubted her. Was he right? Was she a coward?

When she didn't speak, Cloud shrugged and left. She watched him disappear through the deck hatch, his bare feet gripping the ladder rungs, every step slow and stubborn.

Storm let go of the hammock and dropped heavily to the floor. Much later, her uncle found her lying there staring, dry-eyed, at the underdeck. He helped her back into her hammock.

"I want to go above decks."

Uncle whirled round, wagging a finger. "You'll rest until the Healer says otherwise. I've only just picked you up off the floor. Minnow will make my life unbearable if anything happens to you, and well you know it!"

Storm rolled her eyes, but she had to smile at the mention of her young cousin. Uncle was right. When Minnow got an idea in his head he was an unstoppable force. Missing him was the worst part about being at sea for half a year.

Lake returned to his theme: "The Drowned Ones tracked us down. It's a big sea, Storm. No way they just chanced on Yanlin's fleet. We're easy enough to find: the trading routes haven't changed for generations. They want revenge. I think…" Lake cleared his throat. "I think they want you dead, Niece."

It had happened less than a year ago. Using her newly mastered powers over wind and wave, Storm had sunk one of the three raft towns attacking her island. Many Drowned Ones had died. "Yes," she replied. "They came for me."

Lake studied her, black brows knitted over worried eyes, and she winced as she saw possessiveness darken his gaze. She wasn't just his niece – she was a Weather-witch, his most valuable cargo and Yanlin's greatest treasure.

"You're to rest in your hammock until the Healer says you may get up," Lake ordered. "And then you will stay on board this ship. No more sailing off in *Finder*. In a five-day we reach the Inner Sea. The Drowned Ones dare not dirty those waters. You'll be safe enough from them then, but until we reach the Inner Sea, you're ship-bound."

Storm nodded her obedience, only sighing a little in disappointment. Her uncle left quickly, relief flushing his face. *Finder*, the small sailing boat Teanu the Elder had given her, was tied to *Wayfarer*'s stern, bobbing in their wake like a seal pup trailing its mother.

She put a hand to her head and felt her hair, which was gathered into a topknot. When she had been declared the first ever female Weather-witch, her girl's plaits had been cut off and her tunic exchanged for a sleeveless one. Women could not sail with the fleet, so Storm was declared a non-sex, neither male nor female. She would never marry or have children – a fact she had been able to forget on the occasional mornings when she had been allowed to follow the fleet in *Finder*.

It was good, therefore, that she had work to do. The next day, Storm set a cup of water on the floor. She crouched beside it and began to croon a soft, watery tune. All that day and the next, she sent the water spinning round and round inside the cup, first one way, then the other. Her Water-magic had deserted her. She had once again failed her people. Her skills must be at fault. She hadn't been practising hard enough! That would not happen again.

A few days later, as the fleet neared the Inner Sea, Storm was allowed on deck to observe the celebrations. The arrow grazes on her shoulder and leg had grown healthy scabs. Their soreness helped remind her that she had swum close to Death.

"How will you know when the Second Sea stops and the Inner Sea begins?"

"See there?" Lake pointed ahead and slightly to the left. Storm saw a dark pimple on the horizon. "The first of the inner islands, Boabar. A tall mountain sits at its heart, the fires that built it long dead. All sailors navigate by it. When it measures a hand's width above the horizon, we will have entered the Inner Sea."

"And then I can sail *Finder*?"

"And then you can stay on *Wayfarer* and behave yourself!" growled her uncle. "The Inner Sea may be free of Drowned Ones, but it's home to countless privateers, and all of them would love to get their hands on our cargo. The Inner Sea is no place for a green youngster on their own, not even a Weather-witch!"

Storm rubbed her nose in frustration, then went back to drawing in her journal, which she had brought on deck. She was trying to record the attack by the Drowned Ones so she could make it into a story one day, but her fingers were clumsy and stiff and the pictures made no sense. Finally she gave up and simply watched the pimple that was Boabar's mountain grow taller. At last, a cheer rose from the deckhands.

"Foam, take the tiller!" shouted her uncle, and the second master bounded forward and took Lake's place at the tiller. Foam, a short, round, nimble-footed man, gave Storm a knowing grin.

"Follow me, Niece," ordered Lake. "Time to make an offering to the Dolphin!"

Heart thudding, Storm wove her away across the deck after her uncle. Cloud had told her there would be an initiation ceremony for those on their first voyage to the Inner Sea, and she only hoped it would not be too painful or embarrassing. Two boys, this season's apprentices, waited anxiously in the bow of the ship.

"You three, line up in front of me," the captain shouted. "Whelk! Dip the bucket!" As one of the crewmen ran to dip a wooden bucket tied to a rope over the side of the ship, Lake whipped out his knife. "All right, first-timers, hold out your hands."

Storm saw Cloud slip to the front of the assembled crew. He gave her a reassuring nod. He must have decided to forgive her. A knot in her heart eased. Storm gave him a quick smile, trying to look unconcerned about the sharp knife her uncle was holding in a businesslike manner. The two other first-timers stuck out their hands, palms up. Storm took a deep breath and did the same.

"Bucket!" roared the captain. And the bucket appeared, sloshing full of seawater, plonked in front of her uncle, who grabbed the nearest boy's hand and stuck the point of his knife in the fleshy part of the boy's thumb. Storm saw the apprentice wince. Her uncle held the boy's thumb over the bucket, letting his blood fall into the water.

Her turn. Lake was rough but deft. A sharp pain, then she was watching her blood fall – drop-by-red-drop – into the seawater and immediately disappear. She clenched her fingers over her stinging thumb as she watched her uncle do the same to the last of the new apprentices.

The captain held the bucket high, as if it was a prize captured in battle, and the gathered crew gave a cheerful roar of approval. Lake walked to the side of the ship. "Trickster!" he shouted to the seas. "Dolphin! Spirit of Water! Ruler of the Seas! Drink deep on the blood of Yanlin! Greet our newest sailors, who enter the Inner Sea for the first time. Grant them the right to sail upon your Element. Don't trick away their lives, for they have already given you their blood. All this we ask, in the name of the Unknowable One!" And he tilted the bucket of water and blood upside down and poured its contents into the waves.

Storm stood stiffly, sandwiched between the boys. She stared into the water. Her thumb throbbed in time to her heartbeat as she watched the dark shape of a huge creature pass far below, swimming beneath the shadow of the *Wayfarer*.

◄────►

"I wanted a word," said her uncle, carefully extinguishing the lighting stick in the bucket of water beside the door. In the flare of lamplight, he studied her face. They were in the chart room – the captain's sleeping quarters and the only private place aboard ship. "Without your shadow listening in. Although, come to think of it, Cloud hasn't been underfoot lately. You two fallen out?"

"No." Storm shrugged. "Not really."

"Hmph. Wouldn't be a tragedy if you had. He's too focused on you. There's no future there."

Storm found she was offended. "It's not that!"

"Oh?" Lake's eyebrows rose in a questioning curve.

"It's my magic Cloud likes, not me!"

"So that's the way of it? I noticed he fancies playing hero."

"He's angry with me for not sinking the raft town."

"And I'm pleased you didn't kill yourself trying! You're of no worth to Yanlin drowned and eaten by the fishes!"

A proprietorial glint in his eyes. Storm looked away.

"But I didn't bring you here to talk about Cloud. I need to warn you."

She glanced up, wondering.

"The Pact," said Lake, as if that explained everything.

"What about it, Uncle?" Everyone knew about the Pact – the group of fifteen families who ran Bellum Island, where most trading was done.

"They'll be after you."

"After me? I don't understand."

"Witches…" he paused, his jaws working as if he was chewing on something foul tasting, "…don't have to work for their birth island. The Pact will try and win you. Bribe, if you like. So you'll leave us and go work for them. Make them even richer!"

"But I wouldn't!"

He just looked at her, then licked his lips. Sighed. "Teanu said you'd be loyal, but … she's never met Talon. He runs the place, and he's sly, even for a Bellumer. So I'm warning you: don't trust him. Don't trust a one of them. Remember who you are, Storm. Remember Minnow and Dain."

It felt like he had slapped her. After a while she said, "I'm not likely to forget them."

◄———►

One five-day later, they arrived at the centre of the Inner Sea: Bellum Island. Every crew member not actively sailing the ship had gathered on deck. The winds were against them so, at her uncle's request, Storm had magicked a northerly to blow the fleet swiftly over this last leg of their journey. To her relief, her Air-magic, always more reliable than Water, had worked predictably. Now she stood beside Lake and watched the most famous island of them all turn from a faint smudge on the horizon into solid land.

Land, but unlike any island Storm had ever seen. Instead of cliffs, beaches and shoaling rocks, Storm saw a wall of solid lava rising sheer out of the sea. The cliff was the reddish-black colour of burnt grain, and it loomed higher the closer they got until it was taller than two ships stacked one atop the other.

"Ease the northerly!" ordered Lake. "Then a gentle easterly, to help us circumnavigate to starboard."

Storm was full of questions, but she pushed them from her mind for the moment and concentrated on shifting the direction of her wind. What if her magic failed again?

Worrying won't help! snapped her mind-voice.

One by one, the *Wayfarer* in the lead, Yanlin's fleet veered right and began to sail around the enormous cliff encircling Bellum Island.

Storm darted a glance at her uncle. Lake was frowning in concentration as he adjusted the tiller with small, precise movements, keeping the ship in a channel of deep water between the wall and a string of dangerous-looking rocks to their right. She bit her lip, her forehead beading with sweat as she struggled to keep her wind soft and steady. Gentle magic was always the hardest! Behind them, the rest of the fleet followed in their wake, tracing a slow and treacherous path around the island.

Is this place nothing but a lump of lava? Storm wondered. *Is the town perched on the top of the cliff like a gull in its nest? Where is the harbour?* But she didn't dare interrupt her uncle's concentration to ask. Without warning, a trio of three sleek harrier ships appeared in front of them, apparently popping out of solid rock. A dark line appeared in the lava wall, gradually widening to form an opening. The ships had emerged from a tunnel in the lava cliff!

Storm felt a shiver of awe run up her spine. She was looking at the doorway to Bellum Island! Now the legendary wealth and power were explained. Not only was Bellum the belly button of the world, placed as it was at the exact centre of the Inner Sea, but the island itself was a freak of nature, encircled completely by a wall made of hardened lava. These were defences no pirate or Drowned One could ever penetrate.

"Belay the wind!" growled Lake.

Storm let her wind fade and stood, shivering with excitement. One of the harriers launched a small boat crewed by three men. Two rowers sent the boat bouncing across the wave-tops towards them while the passenger in the bow stood once they were within hailing distance.

"Identify yourself!" he shouted. "Island and captain."

"Yanlin. Lake of Yanlin!" her uncle roared back.

The man checked a tally sheet, nodded. "Clear to enter, Lake of Yanlin!" The boat reversed and rowed back towards the harrier.

"Lower the rowing boat!" Lake shouted.

The rowing boat would laboriously pull the *Wayfarer* through the tunnel piercing the cliff, Storm realised. And then the remaining ships, one by one. "Uncle!" she interrupted, wondering at her bravery. "I can take the fleet through."

"Wha—" Her uncle stared blankly at her, then a slow grin spread over his face. "Genius!" he said with a laugh. "Of course you can. Belay that rowing boat!" he roared at the crew, and the men winding the windlass shrugged and cranked the boat back on deck. Eyes wide with delight, Lake said to her, "This'll put a stir into 'em! Yanlin will make a grand entrance. Not to mention the time and sweat you'll save us." He lowered his voice, leaned towards her. "You sure you can do it? It's a narrow tunnel. Narrow and long, and not a breath of wind."

"There will be wind today!" Storm grinned back at him, excited and nervous, but certain of her power. Precise magic, and gentle, but she knew she could do it. She looked up and saw the unmistakable arc of wings far overhead. For the first time since becoming an Air-witch Storm felt pleasure at the sight of the Albatross – and a sense of belonging.

3

Storm knew it would be easier to direct the wind if she followed the fleet. One by one, and with much groaning of timber and clinking of tackle, the other ships eased past.

Air-music was already singing in her veins and pulsing in her head, smooth and cool, light and flowing. A breeze came with her first thought, blowing light and steady. Part of her mind noticed that the sails of the Bellum harrier ships, which lay only a few ship-lengths away, did not so much as flutter. Precise magic indeed! She felt a stir of pride as the stern of the first of Yanlin's ships disappeared from sight into the tunnel, but pride was immediately replaced by panic. What if the tunnel changed direction? If the narrow channel twisted right or left, her wind must shift in turn, or the ships would be left stranded, becalmed.

"Is the tunnel straight?" Storm grabbed at her uncle's arm.

Lake understood at once. "No, by the Ancestors! Halfway along it twists like an eel and doubles back on itself. Shall I sound a warning bell and stop the ship?"

"No. Wait!" Storm glanced at the sky and saw the Albatross near overhead, wings set wide, like twin sails. As she watched the Elemental, Storm saw, as though with a second pair of eyes, a curving canyon below her. She saw a winding path of blue water twisting between red-black walls.

A shiver of joy and fear combined ran up and down her spine. *I am seeing through the eyes of the Albatross itself!* This was magic indeed! It was intoxicating.

"I can see," Storm said. "It's all right." She marvelled that her voice was so calm. With her human eyes, Storm watched the tunnel eat the second ship. At the same time the Elemental spirit showed her the first ship, as it reached a turn in the channel. She adjusted the leading edge of her wind.

Storm guided each ship, following the twists of the tunnel, adjusting her magical wind for each vessel. Her second sight watched the first ship break free of the tunnel and enter the wide blue lake that was the harbour of Bellum Island. One by one, the Yanlin ships passed through the tunnel, making rapid progress. The *Wayfarer* joined the end of the queue. At last her uncle's ship burst out of the confining walls of lava and her two sights became one.

"Cracking!" breathed Lake. "No one will have ever seen anything like that before. And look – the grandees have come themselves to see us arrive. It's the head of the Pact himself! Old Talon, with a welcoming committee." He gripped her arm, pulled her closer and said in a low voice, "Remember my warning – the old spider is spinning his web. Don't get caught!"

Storm looked where her uncle was pointing and saw three bright figures waiting at the end of a great pier, surrounded by a sturdy thicket of drab-coloured soldiers, like a herd of dung beetles guarding rainbow moths. The leaders of Bellum Town, the richest and most powerful people in the world, had come to witness the arrival of Yanlin's new Weather-witch.

She sat at the back of the long rowing boat, behind her uncle, watching Bellum Town grow closer with each heave of the oarsmen. The sun's heat was already scorching, and she welcomed the spray that splashed over the bow. The Pact leaders, waiting on the pier, looked like brightly painted dolls.

Storm clambered out of the rowing boat as soon as it was made fast and followed Lake's broad back up the steep steps carved into the stone pier. As soon as she stepped on to solid ground, the earth seemed to sway beneath her. Storm grabbed the metal handrail until the pier settled into a slightly nauseating roll. So this was what it felt like to lose your land legs!

"Mistress Storm of Yanlin!"

Storm peered around her uncle to blink at the speaker, a tall round-bellied man with long, curling moustaches. He wore an ornate silk robe of gold and green; his feet were encased in narrow leather shoes of brightest carmine, with pointed toes so long they were tied to his ankles with ribbon to keep them from dragging in the dirt. Instead of a topknot, his hair tumbled in ringlets to his shoulders, and the top of his head was submerged beneath a triangular hat made of orange silk. It was wider than his shoulders, and the pink ribbon attached to its crown curled and uncurled in the breeze.

Either side of him stood a woman and a man dressed just as strangely. Lake tugged her forward. Storm's mouth went dry and she bowed deeply.

She noticed, with amazement, that the three Pact grandees were wearing a sort of coloured paste on their faces. They had painted their cheeks pink, and drawn dark lines on their eyelids, and darkened their plucked and arched brows with kohl.

"Mistress Storm!" The man – who must be the dangerous Talon – rolled the words on his tongue as though they were wine. "Welcome to Bellum Town. We are honoured to greet the greatest witch of our generation."

Storm could not help noticing that all three strangers watched her with a greed that even the thick layers of paint could not conceal. "The honour is mine." She fixed a formal smile on her face. "But I am called simply Storm, not Mistress. I am a non-sex."

"As you wish, Honoured Storm. Let me present you to my colleagues. This is Waffa, who keeps the tally books for the whole of the Pact."

The woman stepped forward. Narrow eyes stabbed at Storm.

"And Almond, who has taken himself away from the trading floors to meet you! The youngest member of the Pact."

The second man bowed gracefully, like a dancer, and when he raised his head Storm was struck by the symmetry of his face, made more striking by the blankness of the paint.

Formalities over, Talon continued their conversation: "Your fame precedes you ... Storm. The chanters sing of the sinking of the pirate raft in Yanlin's harbour last season. Is it true they attacked again, during your voyage to the Inner Sea?"

Impressed, Storm said, "Your spies are efficient."

"Of course." His moustaches spread in a grave smile. "We pay them well. And now," said Talon, pressing his hands together, "I offer you the hospitality of my humble home while you are on Bellum Island. My daughter is beside herself with excitement at the idea of meeting you."

Lake had warned her, but Storm had not expected Talon to pounce so soon. "But I could not impose!"

"No imposition, but the highest honour, I assure you."

Custom dictated that she must accept, and Storm found she wanted to go with Talon, to see his grand house and meet his daughter. "My uncle and I would be honoured—"

"Captain Lake will be able to visit you whenever he desires, of course. He will be too busy trading to enjoy our frivolities."

Storm glanced at her uncle. Lake was turning pink with the effort of not scowling. "Thank you," she mumbled. "But I have not brought my things…"

Other than the clothes she wore, Storm had one change of clothing. As she considered her appearance, her face grew hot. Her tunic and trousers were made of coarse hempen cloth, patched and mended, faded with sun and sea spray. She had not given them a thought before now, but suddenly Storm imagined how she must look to Talon and his companions: a peasant in shabby rags.

"No need, Honoured Storm. We will provide everything you might wish. It will be our pleasure!"

"A private word with my niece, Talon, before you whisk her away!" Lake gave a grimace, which some might take for a smile, before grabbing her elbow and tugging her to one side. He glared over his shoulder at the nearest soldiers, and Talon, with an ironic smile, flicked his long red nails. The guards retreated out of earshot.

"Blast the old octopus!" Lake growled, a low grumble of frustration. "He'll try to dazzle you with riches and promises. Believe none of their words! Keep your wits about you, Niece, and meet me in the Merry Whale in a five-day when the sun is six hands risen above the sea. If you can't get away that day, then you must come the next. Make any excuse you must, but meet me at the tavern!"

"Where is it?"

"It's in the centre of town. Ask anyone. And—"

Two guards suddenly loomed behind them, and Lake choked off his words, wheezing in irritation.

"You can continue your conversation when you visit your niece." Talon's voice rang out behind them, musical as a bell. "Any time, Captain Lake, any time. Only do make an appointment at the guardhouse, you know. And now I fear we must leave. It is simply too fatiguing to stand here in the sun one breath longer!"

The guards stepped between them, forcing Lake to let go of Storm's arm. He bowed curtly, turned and stalked back towards the pier. Storm watched him go, feeling a heady mixture of excitement and trepidation. She was living Thorn's dream. Here she was on Bellum Island, belly button of the world! And she was on her own for the first time in her life, without another Yanliner near. And the most important people in the world wanted her company! She felt grown up and important.

Talon gestured that she should walk beside him. The two other grandees stepped back to let them pass, but Storm heard their silken rustle follow close behind. The beetle-brown guards pushed a path through the gathered crowd of townsfolk and sailors as the procession climbed the hill towards the heart of Bellum Town. Storm glanced over her shoulder and had a last glimpse of the *Wayfarer*, bobbing gently at anchor.

4

The procession wound its way up the steep road. After weeks at sea, the smells of the island assaulted Storm: the stink of rotting seaweed; latrines; cook fires; charcoal from a forge. Hanging overhead was the green-resin scent of pine trees and the smokier perfume of the distant jungle. Under everything lay the deep smell of earth itself.

As they climbed, the vast warehouses lining the harbour became long rows of brick houses, the walls plastered yellow, red, blue or pink. It was all so different from Yanlin. Only the seagulls screaming overhead were the same.

Townsfolk crowded everywhere, carrying bundles, pulling carts, dodging and yelling. Soon the road levelled out and the procession travelled along wide streets lined with tall, rich-looking buildings. At last, the procession turned into a square, surrounded on two sides by towering buildings, and on the third by an enormous gatehouse with a tiled roof.

The open space was paved with alternating squares of red stone and yellow brick. To Storm, it looked like a giant gaming board. Only, instead of tokens, the squares were filled with tables and stalls covered in goods: pumpkins, mangoes and melons; fresh fish and dried; scarves and ribbons; boots and belts; knives and whetstones; arrows and bows; ornaments made of shells and beads; embroidered cloth; and lengths of silk dyed all the colours of the rainbow.

"Is it market day?" she asked Talon.

"You mean the stalls? No, they are here every day."

The noise of commerce died at their approach. People turned and stared as Talon's procession marched through the square towards the gatehouse. The huge iron gate was quartered with images of the four Elementals.

The gatehouse guards snapped to attention and hurried to push the gate inward. It swung open with oiled ease.

As Storm passed the coiled image of the Salamander, her left hand crept to cover the scar on her right wrist

– the brand that marked the Fire spirit's last attempt to kill her.

The guardhouse echoed like a cave with the thud of boots. Storm shivered with excitement and awe. Yanlin had never seemed so far away, so small and insignificant. When she saw what lay beyond the gate, Storm's mouth fell open.

"It is beautiful, is it not?" Talon had anticipated her reaction and paused to give her time to take in this extraordinary place.

Like a precious emerald, a garden lay at the heart of the stone and brick town. Gravel paths wove among flowering trees and shrubs to a central pond. The garden oasis was surrounded on three sides by fifteen tall houses built of plaster-covered brick. Each had tall windows opening on to wrought-iron verandas. Balconies overflowed with wisteria, jasmine and roses. The steep roofs were covered in tiles glazed a shimmering blue that echoed the sky.

"That is my house," Talon said, pointing to a large building facing them at the back of the square. "My daughter will be waiting to meet you. Come!"

"How old are these houses?" Storm hurried after him.

"Very old." Talon's moustaches waggled when

he smiled. "My ancestors have lived here for many generations."

Storm blinked in surprise. Talon's words meant that membership in the Fifteen – the trading Pact that ran Bellum Island – was hereditary. On Yanlin seven Elders were elected by popular vote from among all those who had lived long enough to have had a chance of gaining the necessary wisdom.

It seemed dangerous to trust that your descendants would perpetually be both virtuous and wise, but, she thought, there was no arguing with the success of Bellum.

The door of Talon's house was made of teak, its carvings ancient and worn by wind and sun. It creaked open at their approach to reveal a girl of fourteen or fifteen, dressed in a primrose-yellow tunic and white trousers. Her eyes sparkled with intelligence, her nostrils were elegantly flared, and her lips looked ready to smile.

Storm followed the Pact leader into a hall covered with thick mats of rice straw. A tall window opposite the door flooded the space with light. Storm's eyes widened in astonishment. The window was filled with pieces of glass set in lead frames. She had only ever seen glass in the form of beads: tiny smudged blue and greenish pebbles far too expensive to own. Precious glass was so cheap to the Pact that they used it to shut out the wind!

Behind the primrose girl stood a man and a woman dressed in undyed linen. They bowed low as Talon entered the house.

Servants! Storm couldn't help staring at the pair, who kept their eyes carefully downcast. She had heard that Pact members had people living in their houses whose only jobs were to wait upon their masters, bringing them clothes and food, and doing all the cleaning and cooking, but she had hardly believed such tales.

Talon reached out a crimson-spiked hand and his daughter grasped his fingers with a flutter of a yellow silk sleeve. They turned to face Storm, as though waiting for her applause.

Show-offs! said Storm's mind-voice. *Both of them.* But she was entranced in spite of herself.

"Betaan, here is our guest, Yanlin's famous Weather-witch. I am sure the two of you will become fast friends."

Talon's daughter granted Storm a bright smile, then bent her head in greeting. Long plaits of glossy black hair, twined with rose-coloured ribbons, spilled over her shoulders. Storm gazed with longing at the other girl's beautiful hair. When she had been made a non-sex, her cherished plaits, laced with ribbon and as long as her arm, had been cut off and what remained of her hair tied in a topknot. Her neck and shoulders felt suddenly naked. Betaan made her feel too clumsy, too sea-browned, too plainly dressed, too everything!

"Show Storm where she is to live, Daughter," directed Talon. "She will doubtless wish to tidy up for this evening."

Talon clicked his fingers and the male servant darted forward to help him remove his outer robe. The head of the Pact held out his right foot, and the man knelt to untie the toe and remove the shoe. He presented his master with embroidered silk slippers, and Talon scuffed his feet into them.

"I bid you farewell until this evening, Storm," said Talon. "We have arranged a gathering of the Fifteen Families. Betaan will keep you company until then." He gave her a graceful bow and strode off into the interior of the house.

"Come with me." Betaan made the command sound like a request. Her voice was breathy, like a wooden flute. "I'm sure we will become great friends."

Was that a command too? Storm wondered, as she followed Talon's daughter up a flight of stairs.

5

She had never been in a building with more than one floor. Storm climbed the wooden stairs slowly, staring at the paintings covering the walls. They showed people dressed like Talon and his daughter wandering through lush gardens, feasting, riding in gilded palanquins, overseeing the unloading of cargo in Bellum's harbour. Betaan's ancestors, Storm imagined. Those who had lived in this huge, rich house in distant times. It made her heart thump to see dead eyes looking out from the paintings as though they could still see.

Her mother's house, which was hers now, had been built by Dain and Wing upon their marriage. It was only slightly older than Storm herself. And it would die naturally, of rot and decay, probably in her lifetime, for houses on Yanlin were made of simple reeds, thatch and bamboo, with bits of wood scavenged from the shipyard. Not of dead plaster, like this place.

An immortal house. It made her skin creep. But it was beautiful, she had to admit. A person might kill for a house like this.

"This is your room." Talon's daughter watched Storm from behind her face paint as the servant slid past them and pushed open a tall door of carved teak.

The room was as big as her mother's entire house. A rug of knotted silk lay upon waxed floorboards; the sleeping mat was a thick pad on a low platform of carved teak, with linen neck pillows and a silk coverlet. It was wide enough for three! A clothes cupboard stood against one wall, a tall cabinet lacquered a rich dark red. There was a round mirror of polished bronze hanging on one wall, and a simple low table against another, with a kneeling mat in front of it. The window was filled with squares of coloured glass that threw a rainbow on the floor and across one wall, rippling across a picture hung there.

The image showed squares that must be buildings, doubled lines that must be streets. There were images of fountains, warehouses, the harbour with ships floating in it. All surrounded by the lava wall. It was all drawn upon parchment with flowing brown lines and painted with the soft colours of the earth itself.

"What is this?" Storm stood in front of the image and stared, fascinated.

"It's a map." There was a tinge of amusement in Betaan's voice.

"Map?"

"Like a sea chart."

"But why would you need such a thing? Bellum Town isn't enormous and featureless like the sea."

"Not full of treacherous reefs and hidden rocks?"

"Exactly."

"But isn't the map beautiful?"

"It is. Do you know the person who did it?"

Betaan laughed. Storm was being teased, but the mockery was gentle. "The artist died long ago. That is a very old painting. And it was painted out of vanity. Of course we don't need a map of Bellum Town! But one of my ancestors wanted one – wanted to chart the town as it was in her day." Betaan shrugged. "Life isn't about what we need, but what we want."

Storm turned from the map to see Betaan gliding across the room to a second, smaller door. The serving woman darted forward and pushed the door wide.

"Fill the bath," Betaan ordered. The servant bowed and left. "I assume you *would* like a bath? The facilities aboard ship can't be that luxurious."

"It's called going for a swim!" Storm peered through the open door and saw a large bamboo tub on a raised platform in the centre of a small room. "You have inside bathing rooms!" At home they showered outside, under water stored in cisterns.

"Of course! And as for swimming at sea… You are very brave." Betaan looked at her curiously. "But of course, being a Weather-witch…" Talon's daughter gazed pointedly at Storm's topknot. "Do you mind being a non-sex? Your hair, I mean. And never to have children?"

"There is no other way." Storm spoke briskly. Betaan took the hint, merely raising an eyebrow in echo of her father.

The serving woman returned, a bucket of steaming water in each hand. She bustled into the bathing room, poured out the hot water and disappeared again with the buckets. Storm's eyes flew wide. An extravagance of hot water!

"Let's find some fresh clothing!" Betaan swept to the lacquered cupboard and threw open the doors, revealing piles of bright, soft silk. "I had to guess your size and what colours you might like. Come, choose what you would like to wear tonight!" She pulled out tunics and matching trousers and threw them on the bed, a heap of embroidered silk in all the colours of the rainbow.

Storm lifted up a tunic, then another. Her chest felt strangely tight. Even her Choosing tunic, lovingly embroidered by her mother, had not been as beautiful as these garments. She feared to snag the soft fabric with her calloused fingers. She knew, absolutely, that they were not for her, but she desired, oh, how she desired…

The serving woman hurried through the room, poured out more water. Lifted from her daydream, Storm said reluctantly, "These are not suitable."

"Don't you like them?" Betaan drew back.

"It isn't that… They are beautiful. All of them. But … I am a non-sex. These are women's tunics."

"Is that all?" Betaan laughed, her voice pealing with relief. "But that is so provincial. The Pact makes the rules on Bellum. As long as you stay with us, you can be both girl and Weather-witch! Of course, if you prefer, I'll have a seamstress come and alter them – cut the sleeves right off!"

"Oh, you mustn't!" Storm stared at Betaan, horrified. "They're far too beautiful." She hesitated, heart hammering with eagerness. "Is it really true?

Your people would accept a female Weather-witch?"

"Of course! Now choose. You must wear something tonight and, forgive me, but your shipboard clothes will not do." Talon's daughter raised both eyebrows this time, looking disdainfully at Storm's weather-stained tunic and trousers. Storm glanced down at the tumbled clothing. Her agreement with the Yanlin Elders couldn't matter while she was a guest of the Pact. She could be a girl again!

Storm smoothed the front of her tunic, feeling the coarseness of the cloth under her palms. She reached out a tentative hand to stroke a tunic of deepest blue, the colour of the Albatross. "This one. I want to wear this, please." And she sighed with pleasure. Bellum Island was proving more wonderful than she could have imagined.

"The bath is ready, Mistress!" The servant, her face pink with effort, bowed to them.

←———→

Storm had never felt so gloriously clean in all her life. She had been soaped, scrubbed and towelled by the servant, much to her embarrassment. Her hair had been washed three times, oiled and combed. But she couldn't get used to the feeling of it brushing her cheeks and the back of her neck. Betaan had refused to let Storm tie it up again into a topknot. "It's the fashion here, for formal occasions. Besides, you have such lovely hair. It falls in waves, like the sea. Mine is as straight as a stick. You will leave it alone! It will soon grow long enough to plait, if you wish."

"I won't be here that long." She sighed. It might be true, but she wanted to pretend otherwise.

"Don't say that," Betaan said. "Or do you wish to make me sad?"

Storm felt herself smiling at the words.

She doesn't mean it! warned her mind-voice, but Storm pretended not to hear. She followed her hostess down the wide stairs to meet the members of the Pact, revelling in the feel of silk on her skin, tingling with excitement. She pushed Uncle Lake's warnings from her mind. She could stop being Yanlin's Weather-witch for tonight at least. After all, she was about to meet the richest people in the world!

6

They were ushered into a room as tall as two houses. The floor was made of blocks of yellow wood polished until they gleamed. But it was the windows that stole her breath. They reached from the floor to the blood-red ceiling, and their wooden frames were filled with square pieces of clear glass set in lead. The slanting rays of the dying sun flooded through them, and she could see Bellum Town below and around her, warped and shimmering.

"Mistress Storm of Yanlin! Betaan, daughter of Talon!" a servant bellowed.

With silken rustlings, the room turned to face them. Each figure wore a painted mask: pale skin, pink cheeks, black kohl around their eyes. *They do look like wooden dolls*, Storm thought, *but far more frightening!* Both men and women wore their hair loose, falling in oiled locks around their necks.

The room stared back at her in silence as Talon swept into view, swishing between the women and men in their paint and butterfly colours. This evening he wore acid-green. "Ah, Storm, you are come at last. Betaan has such tardy habits!" He cast an affectionate look at his daughter before turning to Storm and bowing with a well-judged mixture of formality and familiarity. "Let me make introductions. The Pact is dying to meet you!"

Talon paraded her around the room. Face after painted face swam into view; words of greeting were murmured, bows exchanged. Storm saw Waffa of the tally sheets rear up and disappear, before a pair of eyes the colour of burnt apricots caught her gaze. Almond, the young trader who had greeted her at the docks, swept forward and bent in a graceful bow.

"Ah, good," said Talon. "Just the person to partner Storm in the dancing. You youngsters go and work up an appetite for the feast I have planned!"

Storm wiped what she knew must be a look of horror from her face. "B-but I am sure I do not know how to dance in your fashion and…" The idea of dancing with Almond, who stood looking at her with barely disguised amusement on his too-perfect face, made her want to sink into the yellow floor.

"Nonsense, Father!" Betaan stepped between them. "Our guest is far too young to dance with an old man like Almond."

Storm felt her eyes open wide at the insult, but an expression of amused tolerance crossed the young trader's face.

"I shall partner Storm this evening." Betaan gave her father an admonishing glance. To Storm she said, "Come and meet my friends."

"Thank you!" Storm gasped as Betaan led her through the crowd. It parted before them as Talon's daughter called out greetings, gathering a group of other girls. Face after painted face turned to study her, and Storm's mouth went dry. What had she to do with these perfect, delicate-looking creatures?

"Gather round and rescue Storm!" Betaan sang out. "She's my new best friend!"

"Lucky Storm," said a tall young woman in a grave voice. Beneath the painted mask, Storm saw a clever and possibly kind face. "I am Mer," said the girl. "I used to be Beta's best friend, but she changes us round weekly." The group giggled. "Welcome!" said Mer.

"Let us dance!" Betaan cried, as the drums began to tap out a rhythm and flutes tootled a catchy tune. She grabbed one of Storm's hands, Mer the other, and in a heartbeat Storm was part of a circle of dancers rotating to the music. If she closed her eyes, she could have been back at home, dancing with Ma and Minnow. Storm let her feet travel the familiar steps, feeling giddy, even reckless. She wasn't Yanlin's Weather-witch now. She was an ordinary girl having fun. *Don't be stupid!* scolded her mind-voice. *If you were an ordinary girl you wouldn't be here. Remember what Lake said about Talon: you cannot trust these people!*

Go away! Storm replied and danced even harder.

←———→

A knocking sound pulled her from an instantly forgotten dream. Storm opened her eyes. Instead of the sea-stained boards of the *Wayfinder* deck an arm's length above her hammock, she saw a gold ceiling high overhead. It took a few amazed heartbeats before she remembered where she was. The knock became an impatient rapping.

"Who is it?" She pushed herself to sitting.

The door flew wide. Betaan marched into the room, carrying a small tray. "Breakfast, sleepy-head! I couldn't wait for you to wake up any longer. I'm dying to gossip about last night. And to tell you about today's excursion." She placed the tray on Storm's lap. It held

48

a tiny teapot, a porcelain cup and a plate of steaming pumpkin rolls. "Eat up! Quickly now."

"Excursion?" Storm poured out tea, took a bite of roll, suddenly famished. It seemed strange to have a whole day before her with no job to do, no task, nothing to make or mend. Work had always come first on Yanlin: she could not remember a time when she had been too young to have any chores.

"I am going to introduce you to the wonders of Bellum Town!" Betaan exclaimed grandly. "Mer will come with us. I think she likes you! But you are *my* best friend, remember?" The other girl tossed off the words with an arch smile.

This is a game she plays. Storm chewed thoughtfully. *And I don't know the rules.*

Her lifelong best friend had been a boy. Thorn had been killed by the Drowned Ones, and she missed him every day. On Yanlin, she had never had a girl friend, only a girl-enemy. *It's a game,* her mind-voice confirmed. *It doesn't mean anything.* But even so, Storm felt a surge of pleasure at Betaan's words and her archly possessive smile.

"I can't wait!" she said. And stole dead Thorn's almost last words: "I've wanted to see Bellum Town my whole life!"

7

"But I can't walk outdoors in these!" Storm stared woefully down at her feet. A servant had brought delicate saffron-coloured leather slippers and showed her how to tie the long toes to her ankles. "The soles are thin as rice wafers. They will wear out within days!"

"And then you get the pleasure of new ones! In a five-day the fashion might be for longer toes, or heels, or no toes at all. What fun, eh? Come, you are no longer stuck on an outer island. Enjoy yourself!" Betaan smiled at her indulgently, but Storm thought she spied a hint of scorn behind the smile. She must be more careful not to appear provincial!

"The shoe-sellers must sell shoes, you know," added Mer.

Storm's face was still warm with embarrassment as

she followed the other two out of the grand front door. But it wasn't Betaan's cheerful teasing or Mer's gentle gaze that made her most uncomfortable. It was the four leathery-brown guards that followed them, with their impassive faces and long iron-clad pikes, watching and listening to everything while pretending not to. Betaan and Mer seemed not even to notice the presence of the three men and one woman.

"Surely we don't need guards!" Storm whispered to Betaan.

"We never go out without guards!" Betaan's eyes grew wide with amazement. "We are the Pact!"

"We might be kidnapped," explained Mer. "All members of the Fifteen Families travel the city with guards."

"Kidnapped? But this is your island! Oh … you mean by visitors, privateers?"

Mer opened her mouth to say something. Storm watched her eyes flick at Betaan, saw Mer shut her mouth.

Betaan turned, smiling. "Of course," Talon's daughter said smoothly. "Privateers, pirates. Everyone comes to Bellum Town to trade, even villains. We are the belly button of the world."

Storm smiled, hiding her confusion. It must be true:

on Yanlin every islander was a member of an extended family. You might have enemies among your own, but they *were* your own. Not even this island – belly button or not – could be that different.

A Pact daughter on each side of her, arms linked in her own, Storm walked through the echoey, sombre guardhouse out into the heart of Bellum Town.

←——————→

The guards went front and behind and the crowded street emptied as if blown clear by Air-magic. Betaan led them from stall to stall. Though only mid-morning, the air was sticky with heat. Palm trees had been planted in clumps across the square, their fringed leaves offering patches of shade. Dust motes danced in columns of light where the sun speared through the leaves. The smell of fried onion and plantain from food stalls mingled with the odour of human sweat and exotic perfumes. Storm's head swam at the richness of it all.

"Perfect!" called Betaan, stopping at a stall selling gold ornaments and gesturing for Storm to join her. She ignored the vendor, a thin old woman sitting in the shade of a canvas tent. Her fingers were so gnarled by arthritis it seemed impossible they had done the intricate work displayed. Storm gave the woman a quick bow and the woman blinked, as though in surprise. After a moment, she bowed in return. Something moved in the tent's shadows. A cling-monkey leapt up on to the woman's shoulder, bending its mouth close to her ear and chattering, its eyes on Storm. Then Talon's daughter spoke, and Storm forgot the monkey.

"This, I think." One long, curving, enamelled fingernail tapped a wrist cuff made of fine gold wires. "What do you think?"

Storm bent closer. The wires had been close-twined and braided to create the image of a seabird soaring over towering waves. "It is beautiful. I have never seen such fine work." *Or so much gold in one ornament!* she thought. *This would keep a family for a year on Yanlin.*

Betaan peered sideways at her. "You like it?"

"Of course. Who would not?"

"Then it is yours." Talon's daughter plucked the bangle from the cloth and, taking hold of Storm's arm, slid the cuff on to her wrist.

Storm stared at her arm, mesmerised. The gold was heavy; smooth, rich-feeling. She glanced at the stallholder, who was watching her with bright eyes set deep in her wrinkled face. Something in her expression reminded Storm of her old teacher and Elder, Teanu.

Disturbed by something she could not put words

to – and by the strength of her own desire for the cuff – Storm blurted: "I cannot accept such an expensive gift!" She pulled off the bangle and held it out. "It is impossible."

"Nonsense!" Betaan shrugged petulantly. "I *want* to give it to you. If you do not wear the trinket, it will lie in the dust. The beggars can have it!"

Storm turned to Mer. "I can never repay such a gesture."

"You are a Weather-witch," Mer said. "You will soon be as rich as any of us. Richer, perhaps. Besides, with Betaan all things are possible. Wear it and enjoy. It costs you nothing to accept, and it gives her pleasure and the old woman profit. Who loses?"

Mer's words were convincing. Storm did not want to spoil Betaan's pleasure. She slipped the cuff back on her wrist. It was a beautiful thing, and it covered the Salamander's scar perfectly. Never had she worn anything half so lovely. She bowed to Talon's daughter, pressing her hands together, unable to stop smiling. "It is beautiful. I will treasure it."

"Good." Betaan lost her marble-like aloofness. "By the Ancestors, that is an ugly scar on your wrist. It is shaped just like a hand. How did you come by it?"

"The scar?" Storm blinked. "I burned myself."

54

"It almost looks like the Salamander had grabbed you by the wrist," Betaan said with a careless laugh.

Storm held her breath, quelling a sudden desire to shiver. Did the Pact know even that horrible secret? But no, it had been meant as a joke. Storm glanced at the stallholder, who was still staring at her intently. The monkey had vanished.

"Gentle daughters of the Pact!" cried the old woman suddenly. "Draw near and I shall entertain you with a special magic, as thanks for your purchase." She addressed Betaan and Mer, but darted a sideways glance at Storm that stirred the hairs on the back of her neck. *Smiths work with fire!* warned her mind-voice.

Betaan laughed, grabbed Storm and Mer by the hands and pulled them forward. "A show! Yes. Give us a show! Are you a witch, old woman? You look like one, to be sure!"

"Don't be rude, Betta!" Mer said, her voice light and careless.

Storm stared at the other girls, deeply shocked. Those who have lived to old age should be honoured, no matter their station in life! It was on the tip of her tongue to say so when Betaan's gasp of amazement made her glance at the stallholder.

The old woman stood behind her table, a coil of fine

wire before her, her hands held out, gnarled fingers waving over the metal.

One end of the gold wire had risen into the air and was twisting and turning like a blind worm. It twisted and coiled, turning back on itself, in and out, knotting and twining until a tiny golden lotus flower stood before them, its circlet of pointed petals supported by a stem of braided gold.

"For you, Mistress!" The old woman snipped the flower stem from the remaining coil of wire and held the trinket out to Betaan, who cupped it in her hands greedily. Even more quickly, a second flower rose from the table and was handed to Mer.

"And for you," said the old woman, looking into Storm's eyes. "Something a bit different." The goldsmith's fingers fluttered like the wings of a humming bird, quicker and quicker, as she wove a spell over the last coil of wire. A shape formed, but not that of a flower. An animal stood on the table – a tiny gold monkey with long arms and tufted ears.

"A cling-monkey!" cried Mer. "How clever."

The old woman held the figure out to Storm, who looked at it warily.

"Are you a Fire-witch?" Storm asked.

"Never!" The old woman chuckled. "I am child

of the Tortoise. Come, let me embrace you, for you remind me of my long-dead daughter."

Still nervous, Storm bent her head towards the old woman. But instead of kissing Storm's cheek, the old woman whispered in her ear: "You are wise to fear the children of Fire! Look for the old man with the monkey. He will help you. Fare you well, Weather-witch, and beware the Salamander's child!" She placed the golden monkey in Storm's hand, then stepped back into her stall and sat on her stool. The show was over.

Talon's daughter turned to the nearest guard. "Pay the woman! She has entertained us well."

The female guard strode to the stallholder and took out a wallet. Storm stowed the old woman's gift carefully in her waist pouch before her companions caught her once more by the hands and pulled her along the streets of Bellum Town.

8

Like the twisting strands of her wrist cuff, side streets led off the central square to smaller ones packed with market stalls, hawkers, jugglers, musicians. Storm's ears were battered with the cries of sellers vying for attention; buyers haggling; minstrels singing and dancing; jugglers crying at the passing crowd to stop, watch, part with a piece of silver. Several times Storm spotted ragged figures being pursued by the crowd to the call of "Thief!"

Stealing was almost unknown on Yanlin. But then, so was insulting the venerable. Her fingers pressed against her waist pouch, feeling for the wire monkey. Why had the old woman warned her to beware the Salamander's child? *A Fire-witch*, replied her mind-voice. *It can be no other.* She pushed the thought away. Worrying would not help. She must simply be careful. Very careful. And find an old man with a monkey!

"Is there much thieving here?" Storm asked her companions, after yet another hue and cry rose above the market sounds, and she spotted a thin, grubby-looking girl of eight or nine struggling in the grasp of a stallholder.

"No more than normal." Mer shrugged.

"What will happen to that child?"

Betaan ignored the question. "Another witch!" she cried, pointing. "I've never known so many in town at once. Let's go and watch." She marched towards a clump of loitering shoppers. The cheers and laughter stopped as the guards pushed through the crowd. Storm's face grew hot with embarrassment as she followed Betaan and Mer to the front.

A thin young man in a sea-green robe stood on the stone ledge surrounding a fountain. The water he had been magicking fell back into the pool with a messy splash as he stared at the guards in alarm.

Ignoring the sullen faces of the townsfolk, Betaan ordered, "Perform well, Water-witch! Today you entertain two daughters of the Pact!"

The young man gazed at them gravely. As his eyes met Storm's, they widened, and he bent his head in a slight bow of acknowledgement. *He knows who I am!* Storm thought. *Like the old woman. But how?*

"Get on with it!" snapped Talon's daughter.

The man straightened in surprise, his face reddening. "I am a visitor to your island and will perform with pleasure although, on my island, patience and good manners are held to be more valuable than magic."

Talon's daughter is spoilt! Her mind-voice was scathing.

She doesn't know any better, Storm replied. *Go away! I want to watch this.* Water-magic was tricksy, like the Dolphin. She needed to concentrate.

The young man dropped his hands to his sides, lifted his head and began to sing a wordless song. The notes rippled and danced in Storm's head. The witch drew a circle in the air. Immediately, the water in the fountain began to rotate, swirling faster and faster. He pointed to the sky, and a long, thin snake of water leapt into the sky where it circled, writhing and dripping.

The crowd cheered. The Water-witch gave an involuntary smile, full of confident joy. Storm felt a twinge of envy: she still had to force herself to trust the Dolphin. Now the young man raised both hands high in the air and fluttered his fingers. The tempo of his song increased; notes trilled from his throat. The water snake split into ten snakelets.

Watery serpents twirled and danced over the square, meeting and disengaging, pairing and parting. The witch began to whistle, a series of playful notes. The ten snakelets flowed into each other and formed... Storm gasped. It was the Dolphin itself! Lithe and sleek, the sun shimmering on its waterspun skin, the Elemental sported overhead, leaping and diving.

The crowd screamed its appreciation as the water-image swooped low, straight at Storm. She flinched. The apparition floated over her head, just out of reach. She could smell the mossy taint of the fountain, see the water swirling and shifting, contained by a magic skin. The Dolphin caught her eye and grinned. It lowered an eyelid in a slow, sly wink. Then leapt into the sky and plummeted towards the empty fountain. Water hit stone with a dull boom. The backwash drenched them all.

The crowd screamed its delight. Even Betaan and Mer were laughing and clapping. Storm saw Talon's daughter order a guard to pay the witch. The woman tossed a handful of bright silver at the Water-witch, but the man ignored it. He stood, motionless, soaked to the skin, his eyes fastened on Storm's face.

"Beware!" She could not possibly hear him over the noise of the crowd, yet the witch's voice was close and clear in her ear: "There is danger for you here. The Salamander sends its most powerful agent against you. Beware the Fire-witch!"

←———→

Talon's daughter spent the rest of the morning buying gifts for herself. Soon the guards were laden with packages: silk scarves; earrings of gold and silver; leather belts and shoes; a fighting stick of precious ebony inlaid with silver.

"I am deadly with a fighting stick!" Talon's daughter stroked the silver inlay. "You bear my bruises many a day, do you not, Mer?"

"I used to." The taller girl pushed her hair back from her forehead, where sweat had melted tiny furrows into the paint. "Until I learned not to fight you. Never accept a challenge from Betaan," she advised Storm gravely. "She is quite good, but she also cheats."

"Liar!" Betaan pretended outrage and motioned the guard to pay for the stick.

"I'm safe. I don't fight with the stick," Storm said. The other girls' banter was a distraction now, not a pleasure. She couldn't forget the Water-witch's warning. A Fire-witch could be stalking her right now! She shivered, wishing she had been able to talk to the young man, but he had scooped up his coins and disappeared before she could approach. "I'm better with a bow and arrows," she explained, fearing her words had seemed abrupt.

"I've heard you're not bad with wind and water!" Betaan tilted her head sideways and peered at Storm with an arch smile.

Something about the smile caused a tiny flicker of irritation. "I wouldn't be here otherwise." Storm held out her bangled arm. "Nor would you have given me this." The cuff glinted in a shaft of sunlight and Storm felt suddenly ashamed. She knew these girls were befriending her because of her power, not because they liked her, but sometimes the truth was best left unsaid. She glanced about, looking for a distraction. "Oh, look there!" And hurried over to a stall selling knives.

Storm had given her father's old knife to Nim, the Drowned One boy, in a moment of pity she knew she would regret for the rest of her life. She bowed to the stallholder, a woman of middle years, perhaps thirty. The woman bowed back, but made no greeting. Her eyes were wary. Storm was getting used to it, but she was beginning to wonder about how the rest of the inhabitants of Bellum Island felt about the Pact.

She bent over the table and forgot the teeming crowd, her impossibly elegant companions, the leathery guards watching and waiting. A knife had caught her eyes. It was similar to her father's old knife, but far finer. The bone handle was plain but for a band of silver wrapping the hilt where the bone had been split to take the iron. But the blade of the knife – she saw at once – was the work of a master craftswoman. This blade had been forged and forged again. It had met the fire many times, and its edge was deadly and pure. Then she saw it: an image near the hilt, stamped into the hot metal as it cooled the final time – the image of a Dolphin. Storm caught her breath.

"How much?" She raised her head to find the stallholder studying her.

"You are the Weather-witch."

It was not a question so Storm did not bother to reply beyond a quick smile. She picked up the knife almost reluctantly, fearful that it would prove less than it seemed on close inspection. The hilt fitted her hand as if made for it; the weighting of blade and hilt was perfect.

The Dolphin had taken her father from her when she was five. It had taken the rest of her life to forgive the Elemental and accept its magic. This knife held them both: the Trickster she had feared and the father she had loved.

"Please, how much?"

"You want that?" Betaan was peering over her shoulder. "It's very plain."

Storm ignored the dismissive note in the other girl's voice.

"How much?"

"No price." The stallholder was looking at her. She did not seem to see the daughters of the Pact, did not bow or retreat into the dimness of her tent. It was as if she and Storm were alone. "For you, no price. Take it!"

"I cannot. It is work of the highest quality. You must have payment."

"You are the Weather-witch. It bears your sign. Take it. But remember this place, this island, our people. Remember us!"

She heard Betaan draw in her breath sharply. "Where has she gone?"

The woman had melted into the darkness of her tent.

"After her!" Talon's daughter gestured to the guards, who stood gaping, laden down and unable to give chase without dumping her purchases on the ground where they might be stolen or trampled. When a guard finally pushed the flap aside, there was no one within.

"Leave it!" Mer put a restraining hand on Betaan's

arm. "There is no harm done. We will mark the stall; the trader will doubtless return."

Did she say "trader" or … "traitor"? Storm stared at her companions, trying to make sense of the scene. Her fist tightened around the knife's hilt. First the other witches' warnings, now this sign of something amiss on Bellum Island. *What was going on?*

"Time to return, I think." Mer had taken charge, giving Betaan a little shake. Talon's daughter seemed to come out of a spell. She turned to Storm, a stiff smile spreading her lips. "Mer is right. We will go home. We have enough purchases today."

"You have, you mean!" Mer laughed. "We have bought nothing."

"What am I to do with this?" Storm stared at the knife in her hand. She wanted it desperately.

"Leave it!" Betaan's voice was sharp. "It is a plain, poor thing."

"It is plain, yes," said Mer, "but nonetheless beautiful for that. Keep it, if you wish. The woman gave it to you."

"Because I am a Weather-witch?" Storm frowned. "I don't understand." But her mind-voice remembered: *Not "a" Weather-witch. She said "the" Weather-witch.*

9

Storm excused herself from yet another formal dinner as soon as she could, pleading tiredness. Days spent doing nothing but eating and shopping were surprisingly exhausting! There had been no sign of an elderly man with a pet monkey in the crowds. But then, neither had she spotted a Fire-witch among the dozens of witches she had seen entertaining shoppers and seamen for a handful of silver. She had not been given any more mysterious messages, but the sense of being watched – and not just by Talon's guards – increased day by day.

Storm slipped away from the crowded gathering room, murmuring apologies to Talon and his daughter, nodding farewell to the dozen guests whose names she couldn't remember.

She escaped into the rear courtyard and out through the ancient wooden gate that led on to an expanse of communal garden. Like the formal garden in the central square, the rear garden served all the houses of the Pact, wrapping round them. Betaan had boasted that it was nearly as large as the town itself, extending to the sea cliff that fell away into the distant harbour.

She wandered neatly tended paths for a long time, planning how she would escape to the tavern long enough to speak to Uncle. Tomorrow it would be a five-day since she had come to live with the Pact. Storm glanced towards Talon's house and spotted a guard standing at the gate, watching her. Storm sighed, turned her back and strode deeper into the mock wilderness.

She soon forgot the watcher. The sound of water was everywhere, trickling from pond to pond, running in shallow rivulets between flower beds. Songbirds trilled, singing all the more frantically as the sun sank towards the sea. Butterflies flirted in fading pools of sunshine.

Storm paused in the middle of a wooden bridge leading from one flower-strewn mini-island to another. *How Ma would have loved this place!* For the first time since Dain's death, Storm felt a strange comfort at the memory of her mother. She wandered towards the cliff edge, found a bench perfectly placed and sat down to watch the sun sink into the sea.

Why have so many witches travelled to Bellum Island? But she thought she knew: the Dolphin, Tortoise and Albatross had sent them because the Salamander's most powerful witch was here to kill her. The very fact that she hadn't yet seen one Fire-witch in the town was worrying.

She pulled the tiny gold monkey from her waist pouch and examined it. "Seek out the old man with the monkey," the goldsmith had said. If she found the old man, would he know the answers to these riddles?

"I'm not afraid," Storm told the setting sun. It was a lie. Why had the Elementals singled her out to wield power over both Water and Air? Why did the Salamander want her dead? "I'm only me!" she whispered to the dusk, feeling very young, very alone and not particularly brave. "Tortoise? Are you there?"

The Elemental was silent, but a ke-ke bird flew to perch on a stem of fragrant wisteria above her bench and began to sing. It sang the sun down. Her heart slightly eased, Storm returned to her too-large room and too-soft bed. The moon rose and set again before she slept.

←——→

"How nice you look!" Betaan stood back, examining

her handiwork. "Don't you agree, Mer?" The morning sun slanted through the glass of the window and showed Storm an image of herself in the brass mirror that both confused and pleased her.

"Absolutely." Mer smiled at Storm. "You might start a fashion for short hair. And Beta has done a good job with the cosmetic. Your eyes look huge now."

"I still want to pluck your eyebrows," Betaan said. "They make you look fierce."

"I like my brows. Perhaps I am fierce." Storm stared into the mirror, and her heart beat faster at the sight that met her eyes. The translucent layer of paint made her eyes, mouth and hair look dramatically dark. *Can that be me? I look … exotic. Exciting even.* When Betaan had insisted on painting Storm's face, she had decided it would be quicker to give in. Storm needed to go to town early this morning in order to escape her custodians in time, or Uncle Lake would wait at the inn in vain.

"Almond will certainly want to dance with you next time!" Betaan gazed at Storm through half-lowered eyelids, and Storm felt her face grow warm.

"I am too young to dance with a grown man."

"True. But in two years you will be a woman, and if you stay with us, you will be able to *be* a woman, not a non-sex. You would be able to marry, to have children.

70

Don't you want a family some day? Why should you sacrifice yourself for your island?"

Not answering would be rude. Storm spoke reluctantly: "Weather-witches have always been men. Some of the Elders worried about the Balance." The hardest thing about being Chosen by the Elementals had been becoming a non-sex. But she had made the choice, done what her Elders demanded. "Everyone makes sacrifices for their people."

"I don't." Talon's daughter stared at her. "Why should I? This is my only life on this earth, and I intend to enjoy it. Besides, your Elders' demand was unreasonable. Oh well, your island is small and isolated. I suppose your people cannot avoid being superstitious and uneducated. The Elementals gave you your powers, so how can it be wrong?"

"Our people are no less educated than yours!" Betaan shouldn't call Yanlin small and isolated – even if it was. "Our chanters know all the old tales. And we do not have as many thieves as you suffer. And—"

"Of course your chanters are excellent," Mer soothed. "Betaan often speaks before she thinks. But she is proud of Bellum, as we all are. And you, of course, are proud of Yanlin. But you cannot live as a woman if you return to your island."

Storm inclined her head, acknowledging the truth of Mer's words. "I must give my life to my people," she said. "I am a Weather-witch. I have no choice."

"You do!" Betaan grabbed Storm's hands, eyes large and pleading. "Stay here with us. Live as we do. Be whomever you like. Enjoy your life. You did not ask to be a Weather-witch, so why should you suffer for the actions of the Elemental spirits?"

"I don't know." Betaan's pleading expression was so un-Betaan-like that Storm wanted to laugh. She heard once again the words of the Albatross, spoken on the day of her Choosing: *Storm-bringer. Storm-rider. Storm-queller. Much is needed from you. Learn what it is.* "We cannot always choose our life's path."

The other two girls exchanged a glance. Betaan shrugged. "Here," she said. "Put on these earrings I bought for you yesterday. And then we will go into town to visit my favourite tea shop. I shall treat you to the best plum cakes in the Inner Sea!"

The sun was already three hands above the horizon when they set out, the usual guards in attendance. Storm's stomach knotted with nerves. The morning would soon pass and much depended on luck ... and these guards. They were the same three men and a woman as on previous days.

"What are their names?" Storm asked her companions, whispering to avoid giving offence to the guards.

"Names?" Betaan looked blank. "You!" She pointed at the nearest guard, the woman. "The Honourable Storm wishes to know your name."

"Tolbar, Mistress." A frown flitted across the woman's usually impassive face.

"Shall I ask the others?" Betaan turned to Storm with a patient expression.

"No." Storm watched the guard. The woman's face remained wooden. She looked clever – possibly too clever – but time was running out. Storm had promised to meet Uncle Lake. *Ancestors help me!* Suddenly, her plan seemed anything but foolproof.

IO

They sat at a table in the tea house's small garden, tucked away in one of the many squares somewhere in the south of the city, far from the harbour. Palm trees dangled leaves overhead, splashing welcome shade across the terrace. Bird cages hung from every tree, painted bright pink, blue and yellow. Imprisoned ke-ke birds sang frantically, until Storm's head began to ache.

Her mind-voice muttered irritably: *The song of the ke-ke should be a rare gift from the Tortoise, chanced upon in a forest glade.* She longed to open the cages and let the birds fly free, but she did not dare. Instead, Storm stared at the half-eaten pastry in front of her and felt slightly sick. It was time.

"Have more tea!" Betaan poured perfumed liquid into their cups. It was delicious, but Storm had drunk four cups, eaten three and a half pastries.

"You must excuse me." She rose to her feet. "Please, don't get up. I will return shortly, but I am feeling slightly unwell. The latrine…"

"Ah, poor you," cried Betaan. "Not used to rich food, I suppose. Landlady!" At once, the old woman who ran the tea shop appeared, hands clasped tightly.

"Yes, Mistress?" The old woman bowed deeply, then, as if fearing she had not been obsequious enough, bowed even lower.

"Show my friend to the necessary! Guard, go with her." Betaan motioned to the woman guard, and Storm kept her face frozen in an apologetic smile to hide her disappointment. Well, she had not expected it to be easy.

"Left down the street and along to the city wall, Honoured Mistress," the shop owner said, pointing out of the doorway of her tea shop with a long, tea-stained fingernail.

"If you will lead, Mistress." The guard motioned to Storm.

"Oh," Storm said, with a helpless smile. "The city is so big and scary. I would prefer to follow you, Tolbar, if you don't mind."

The guard stared at her, obviously disconcerted that

Storm had called her by her name. "Um, if you want."
For a moment, she looked like a person instead of a
function. Then the mask dropped: "Just keep close!"

"I will." Storm felt guilty already. Would the woman
be punished? But she had to meet Lake, and this was
the only way…

The street was long, twisting, and crowded. At
first, Tolbar kept turning around to make sure that
Storm was at her heels, but soon the checks became
less frequent. As they neared a crossroads where two
alleys led in opposite directions, Storm dropped further
back. The ever-present crowd thickened around them
helpfully. Tolbar continued past the crossroads, but
Storm darted into the left-hand passage and ran for
her life. She prayed to the Ancestors that the guard
would not look back for a few breaths yet, and that
when she did, the crowd would delay her search. *Please!*
Storm prayed. *Let her choose the right-hand alley!* And then
she was too busy dodging past strangers and trying
to remember the way to the main square to think of
anything else.

←———→

The Merry Whale was an old twisted timber building
on a narrow street a few hundred paces from the main
square. Storm had had to ask three people for directions

before she found it.

Uncle and Foam were seated in a corner of the dark, low-ceilinged main room. Lake glanced at her as she entered but looked away. *Was Uncle being cautious? Or was there danger?* Storm studied the room, but there was no sign of Talon's people. So she bowed politely to the proprietress and made her way to their corner. Storm eased herself on to the mat beside her uncle and he glanced up, surprise on his face.

"Greetings, Uncle. And to you, Foam." She bowed politely to both men and tried to quell her nerves. Her back was to the door, which made her shoulder blades twitch. If Tolbar had managed to follow her trail she might burst in at any moment!

Uncle Lake was still staring at her in amazement. "Is that you, Niece?"

Storm had forgotten; now she felt herself blush. "It's the face paint. Talon's daughter wanted me to wear it this morning and it seemed rude to refuse."

"You grow used to the ways of the Pact then?" Lake's voice was quiet, and that was strange. Her uncle was loud and definite. "You like fancy clothes and painted faces?"

Storm blinked. What was wrong?

"That wrist cuff and those earrings. Solid gold from

77

the looks of them. Who paid for those, Storm?"

"They were gifts." Why was Uncle trying to make her feel bad? It wasn't her fault Betaan insisted on giving her presents.

"You wear girl's clothes again." Foam joined in, his voice also accusing. "Your hair is loose. Have you forgotten your pledge to the Elders? To Yanlin?"

"I forget nothing! When am I allowed to? I'm not here to talk about what I'm wearing or whether there is paint on my face. I am here to hear your news and tell you mine, unless you wish me to return to the Pact now?"

She was a Weather-witch now, not a child to be rebuked. Lake and Foam were being unfair. Or were they? *I have nothing to feel guilty about!* she raged at her mind-voice, which wisely kept silent.

Anxiety flickered to life in her uncle's eyes. "No, Niece. I do not wish you to return to the Pact. I am sorry if I misspoke. It is because I am afraid that we will lose you. You must realise that."

"Do you question my loyalty?" Her anger would not be quelled so easily.

"Do we have reason to?" Foam was not frightened. He looked at her and it was as though her former mistress, Elder Teanu, was rebuking her.

Storm's anger stuttered. "Of course not!"

"You are not a fool," said Foam. "You must recognise the enticements they throw at you. Not just fine clothes and jewels, rich food and luxurious houses. But power of a sort we do not use on Yanlin. Have you not noticed, Storm, how poor the ordinary people are? That here there are masters and those mastered?"

The unease she had felt since arriving on Bellum grew stronger.

"Bellumers don't even make any more!" added Foam. "In the old days – because they didn't need a fleet – both the men and women of Bellum Island were makers. But they haven't produced goods for generations. They merely consume what the rest of us make. If the other islands were to organise and refuse to trade, Bellum would starve!"

"They don't *make*?" Storm stared at her uncle and Foam. How could an island's people not create? Making was life.

"Oh, a few artisan-makers still work on Bellum," replied Lake. "But most of the stalls are filled with goods from other islands."

"But … what do the people do?"

"Survive as best they can," Foam said. "The ordinary folk garden, hunt and fish to scrape a living. Those in

79

town serve the Pact in some way, offering luxuries and distractions for the head families. They run taverns like this for the fleet men. And other things…"

"What other things?" Storm asked, but Foam blushed and looked into his cup of rice wine.

"Teanu gave me a message for you," said Lake.

"A message? Why did she not tell me it herself?"

"It was for a time such as this. The Elder knew the Pact would try to seduce you. She knew they would offer you your gender back. She said, 'Tell Storm to be patient and to trust me. All is possible given time and good fortune.'"

"That is all?"

"No. She said that you must let the Earth spirit guide you. She thinks you have a special connection to Earth because of Dain, that the Tortoise took you as its child because it foresaw your mother's death."

Storm heard again the Tortoise's words: *In choosing life you will find death, but if you turn to death, you and yours will die in turn.*

Last year, in a moment of weakness, she had allowed herself to think of Nim, the Drowned One boy, as a human being instead of her mortal enemy. He had shipwrecked himself on Yanlin and been near to death when she found him. Instead of reporting him to the

Elders, she had nursed the pirate boy back to health. And Nim had repaid her by helping his people attack Yanlin.

With a rising horror, Storm understood that the Tortoise had known that if she saved the Drowned One boy, her mother would die.

II

"Storm?"

Both men were watching her.

"I do not have a special connection to the spirit of the Earth! Enough of this! Talon has set spies to keep watch over me. I managed to escape for a time, but they will find me again soon." Storm longed to tell her uncle about the Water-witch's warning. But what good would it do? Lake could not protect her from a Fire-witch. He didn't even know that the Salamander was trying to kill her. Only Teanu, her island's head Elder, knew about that. And she had sworn Storm to secrecy.

"Then I must ask you what you intend, Niece," said her uncle. "Our trading will be done here in another five-day. Will you be coming with us when we sail?"

Lake's eyes were fastened on her face; his expression that of a man expecting a blow.

"Of course I will be sailing with you!" Storm put her hand over the cuff on her right wrist, over the scar. The idea of leaving Bellum so soon was upsetting – she realised she would miss Mer, even Betaan. Miss the excitement of Bellum Town. And ... the pit of her stomach clenched as she thought about binding her hair into a topknot again and donning the ugly, sleeveless tunic of a non-sex.

"They will try to keep me," Storm said, knowing it to be true. "They won't just let me leave with the fleet. We will have to trick them."

"Have care!" hissed Lake. "I don't trust the woman who runs this place."

"Trusting anyone in Bellum Town is never wise," agreed Foam.

"So it would be well to speak softly." Lake leaned closer, his voice so quiet Storm could barely make out the words. "I agree. The Pact has not had a Weather-witch in many generations, and they want both the power and prestige such magic brings. They will make you work for them by fair means or foul. I will make plans for your escape. But we must finish trading first."

Storm nodded. Trade was essential, or many on Yanlin would go hungry during the coming monsoon.

"I am sorry I doubted your loyalty," Lake said gruffly. "Teanu will see that you don't have to sacrifice everything for Yanlin, never fear. You must come home, Niece!" Lake recovered himself enough to attempt a half-hearted laugh. "Haven't I told you what Minnow will do to me if I return without his beloved cousin?" He gave her arm a clumsy pat. "Can you meet us here again in a five-day?"

"I will try, but after today it will be more difficult to escape the guards."

"We will come to Talon's house if necessary, though we cannot speak freely there. A five-day, at the same time, if you can! Take care, Storm. Be wary. I have a bad feeling in my bones."

"That's just your rheumatism!" Foam attempted one of his jokes. But Storm noticed he looked as worried as his captain as he left with Lake.

Storm watched them vanish into the dim, smoky light of the tavern. She sat, thinking, barely aware of the noise of the other customers, eating, drinking, joking, arguing.

If there really was a Fire-witch on Bellum intent on killing her, then the sooner she left the island the better. But was she ready to return to her life as Yanlin's Weather-witch, to life as a non-sex?

She missed Thorn more than ever. Visiting Bellum Island had been his life's dream. Instead of returning immediately to the tea shop, she would find a gift to lay at his grave in the cave of the Ancestors. Storm bowed her thanks to the proprietress and walked out into the heat, noise and bustle. She pushed the thought of a Fire-witch firmly from her mind. She was on a mission!

Storm visited stall after stall, looking for something special enough for Thorn's ghost. Something to give him pleasure in the afterlife. At last she found it in a small stall in a tiny square. The stallholder was an ancient woman, bent as a fishing hook, who carved toy boats from driftwood and painted them in unexpected colours. Thorn had been Chosen by Water and had loved sailing above all things. The moment Storm saw the boat, she knew.

It was a twin-masted ship: a seagoing vessel that could be sailed single-handed if the sailor was skilled enough. Its sails were golden as the sun, made of fine linen and sewn with thread so delicate she could hardly see the stitches. The mast, keel and rudder were dark blue-grey, and the rest of the boat was painted in pale green, like a heron's egg. Storm picked the toy up in a careful hand, saw the tiny cast-iron anchor lying on coiled rope, ready for use; marvelled at rope rigging so finely twined she could not see how human fingers could have made it.

Storm held the boat out to the old woman, who was watching her, her head twisted up sideways because of her bent back. The woman's eyes were as sharp as splinters.

Storm bowed politely. "May I purchase this, please?"

"You have not asked the price," said the old woman.

Storm's heart sank. She had not thought the boat might be beyond her means to purchase. Of course, something so fine would cost much more than four silver pieces and a few coppers, which was all she had. "Please, Madam," she said haltingly. "Tell me your best price. I want it for a grave gift."

"Ah," said the woman. "That might make a difference. Tell me, was the dead one a good sailor?"

Storm nodded. "The best of us all."

"In that case, how much money have you?"

Storm fumbled at her neck, drew forth her money pouch and held it out to the woman with shaking fingers. "It is not nearly enough," she said in a sad voice. "You are an artist without equal."

"Ha." Nimble fingers snatched the pouch from her.

"Stop bowing, girl. You are a witch and should not bow to the likes of me. The Weather-witch of Yanlin, in fact."

Storm realised her mouth was open and quickly shut it.

"Gossip is what Bellum trades in most of all." The old woman raised a sarcastic eyebrow. "And my art comes from a lifetime learning through hard work and mistakes." She poured out the contents of the money pouch on to the table, counted out the pieces of metal with a thin, crooked finger. "As it happens, this is exactly the price of the boat. I will wrap it in rice paper for you. Mind you look after it until you get it back to Yanlin."

"Thank you! And I will, I promise! You are kind."

"Nonsense!" The woman busied herself, grumbling as she wrapped the stiff paper around the boat and tied it up with string. Storm had to stop herself bowing again in thanks.

"This boat was made with love and will be given with love," said the woman, tying the last knot. "That is more important to me than how many silver coins you pay. How much is my soul worth?" She pushed the parcel into Storm's hands. "I believe that when you make something good and true, you put a part of yourself inside it that stays there forever."

Storm gasped.

"Now what is the matter?"

"Nothing. Only … someone else said that to me."

"And they are dead."

Storm, staring into the past, saw her mother's face.

"Live for them then, child. And for me. For all of us."
And she held out the boat. Storm took it, turned and
walked away down the narrow twisting street, carrying
a piece of the old woman's dreams with her.

I2

She slipped and slid over the pavement, clutching her boat. The street grew even more crowded. Strangers pushed close, blocked her path. Carts trundled; street sweepers darted, swinging brooms like weapons; stallholders shouted; buyers scolded. Storm realised she had lost her way.

She didn't know this small, dirty square or even which wrong turn had led her here. The houses wore peeling paint and holes in their tiled roofs. The townsfolk were equally patched and stained. She saw beggars crouching in doorways, men and women loitering in alleyways. Crew on shore leave crowded the streets, some obviously drunk. The townsfolk stared at her in surprise – her face paint and silken robes marking her as a daughter of the Pact – before looking quickly away, but a few sailors called to her with words that made her blush and hurry on.

Storm was about to turn back and try to retrace her path when she spotted her shipmate Cloud with a group of young men. They were bent over a gaming table in a corner of the square. Here was a bit of luck! Cloud would know the way to the main square. She drew near and stood watching as Cloud took his turn playing at roll bones, laughing and gossiping with the others. When his turn ended, she called, "Cloud! Hello. May I speak with you?"

"Storm?" He turned and stared at her. "Is that really you? You look … different. A real Bellum Town belle."

Storm winced. She should never have let Betaan paint her face. "I'm lost. Can you show me the way back to the centre of town?"

"Well, sure … in a moment. I'm winning, you see. Why don't you join us? I was just talking about you." The others were staring. She saw disbelief, bemusement, excitement, curiosity and – most worrying of all – hostility. Curse Cloud! He had told these strangers that she was a Weather-witch. Yanlin's good fortune was ill luck for other islands. Best to leave, and quickly.

Storm turned on her heel, but before she had gone more than a few paces, she heard Cloud calling after her. He caught up and darted in front of her.

"What's wrong? They just want to meet a Weather-witch."

"Hold on, Yanliner! You been telling a pack of lies?" A big sailor, a head taller than either of them, advanced. The other gamers left the table and encircled them.

"Ancestors!" muttered Cloud. "See what you've done?"

"Me?" Storm snapped. "This is your fault!"

One of the men pushed Cloud, who sprawled forward on his hands and knees. He scrambled to his feet, swearing and lunged at his attacker. Two men grabbed him and twisted his arms behind his back.

"Cowards!" shouted Cloud. "Fight fair!" But his captors just laughed.

The first man advanced until he was nose to nose with Storm. "What are you, girl? A stuck-up Bellum belle or a Yanlin witch?" He grabbed her arm and squeezed hard. His breath stank of alcohol.

"Let go of me or you'll find out!"

The man just grinned and held on. He was hurting her arm.

Patience lost, Storm gathered her Air-magic. The music that lived in the Air shrilled in her ears. Ready! She focused a blast of wind towards the gaming table.

Pressure built in her mind; the shrill became a painful shriek. Now!

A slender but fierce gust whistled through the square. It struck the table squarely, spinning it on one leg, dancing it across the square. Tokens and roll bones sprayed in all directions. Not bad! By luck or increasing skill, she had controlled her magic nicely this time.

The table-master, who had been watching the confrontation with lazy amusement, began to shout and curse. The sailor still held Storm's arm, so she drew in a deep breath, breathed it out in a twisting curling sigh, and watched with satisfaction as a tiny whirlwind lifted the table high into the air. Storm sucked the whirlwind away. The table crashed to earth in an explosion of wood that knocked three sailors to the ground.

The man holding her let go at once, his face pale. Storm stepped back, rubbing her arm. "That answers your question: I'm a witch. And if you don't want me to blow you into the next life, I suggest you go away and leave us alone!"

The drunk looked at the broken table … looked back at her … took a step backwards.

"Let go of him!" she shouted at the men holding Cloud, and they dropped his arms and backed away.

"Come on," Storm said to Cloud. "Or stay with your

friends. I don't care."

←——————→

"The main square is the other way." Cloud had been following her at a safe distance for at least three hundred heartbeats. Storm marched down one street, then another, paying no attention to where she was going, too angry to speak.

"I'm sorry! I screwed up." Cloud sighed loudly. "Will you talk to me, please? And the main square is the other way. If you really want to go there. I don't mind. We can go somewhere else."

"Don't *ever* brag about me to strangers again!"

"I won't. Sorry."

"I don't belong to you. I don't belong to anyone!" Storm knew it was a lie. She seemed to belong to almost everyone – except herself.

"Sorry. Really. It's just…" Cloud sighed. "No. No excuses. I was an idiot. I was trying to get attention. It made me feel more important, which is… Well, it's pathetic. It won't happen again."

Storm lurched to a stop, whirled round. The expression on his face made her want to laugh and cry at once. "Don't worry, I'm not going to blast you. That was a handsome apology. I accept."

The tension went out of Cloud's face. "Friends?"

Storm nodded. "I could use a good friend right now."

"You've got one." He examined her. "You showed those idiots. Now, that is how to use Air-magic! Ancestors! I'm jealous." He grinned, as if to make it a joke. Only Storm knew it wasn't.

"You want to talk about what's bothering you?" Cloud asked.

Storm rubbed her nose in frustration. She couldn't tell him about the Fire-witch. Teanu had been clear: the Salamander's attacks must remain secret. She examined her parcel, knowing she was delaying: the boat was fine.

Storm knew she should return to the Pact until Lake finished trading, but her heart sank at the thought. Until now, she hadn't realised how oppressive the constant surveillance had become. Besides, perhaps today was the day she would meet an old man with a monkey. He must be in town somewhere – there had been something about the old goldsmith that made Storm trust her. She came to a decision. "I don't want to go back to the main square after all. Not yet. Let's go see if we can find some witches performing."

"That's more like it!" Cloud's face lit up. "Let's go find some magic. This way, I think." He pointed back the way they had come.

They walked side by side. After a few more twisting alleys, the streets grew wider, the houses more prosperous looking, and Storm found herself in a square crowded with market stalls and sightseers. She scanned the crowd, looking for the elusive old man, and spotted a group of guards pouring into the square. The leader was Tolbar. The guard's eyes met Storm's.

Overwhelming as a tsunami, determination flooded through her. She had an old man and a monkey to find. Besides, she was cursed if she would allow herself to be harried and followed, kept virtual prisoner by the Pact and their servants!

"Follow me," she hissed to Cloud. "And keep up!" Cloud stared in amazement, and Storm laughed. Recklessness flooded through her veins. "Follow, or go back to the *Wayfarer* now and keep out of trouble! Choose!" She wrinkled her nose at him, wheeled around and darted for the nearest alley, feeling ridiculously cheerful.

She didn't know where she was going and didn't care. But she would lose Tolbar and the other guards if it was the last thing she ever did! As Storm began to run in earnest, she heard shouts behind them. Talon's guards were giving chase.

13

Storm trotted from one alley into another, and another. Cloud caught up and ran beside her. She gave him a cheeky grin, then slid without warning into a cut-through and took to her heels, praying she hadn't chosen a dead end. She heard Cloud swearing and panting behind her as he sprinted to catch up.

Storm was one of Yanlin's best runners. Now she stretched her legs as the alley opened up into a proper street. She hadn't been able to run for weeks and weeks. Despite the heat of the afternoon, it felt glorious!

She dodged through the crowd as fast as she could; darted down a likely-looking side street, took a left, a right, another right, and found herself sprinting up a narrow winding street of tall, thin houses. The houses gave welcome shade. Sweat was pouring off her. It was too hot to run like this much further.

The street narrowed, looped on itself and opened out into a wider space. With a jolt of recognition, Storm slid to a stop. She had somehow circled back to the centre of town: the main square lay dead ahead. She leaned against a shaded wall to catch her breath and placed the boat carefully on the ground. Cloud arrived, and Storm jerked her parcel out of harm's way as he thudded into the wall and slid to the ground where he sat gasping like a stranded fish. A sweaty fish.

"Are you done then?" he asked, when he could talk.

"We lost them."

"I nearly lost my stomach as well! And who are 'them'?"

She just smiled at him. She had Thorn's boat, a golden monkey and, for a little while, freedom.

"You aren't going to tell me, are you?"

"No." She tugged the wire monkey from her waist pouch and held it in her hand.

"What's that?"

"A gift. I think the old woman must have been an Earth-witch. She made it with magic.

"For you?"

"Yes."

"Why?"

Storm stared at the tiny statue. It could not tell her, no matter how lifelike it looked. "I'm not sure yet." She stowed the toy away. "Come on, let's explore." She would search every street in Bellum Town until she found an old man with a monkey.

←——————→

They wandered among the crowd of shoppers and sightseers, which grew thicker as they got nearer the centre of the square, until they could barely push a way through.

Cloud suddenly stopped. "What's that?" He pointed. Over the bobbing heads of the crowd, Storm saw the red canvas of an enormous tent.

"Let's take a look." She was still worried about a Fire-witch, but it was safer to be part of a crowd, and there was less chance of being spotted by Talon's guards. "At least we'll be out of the sun in there."

They squeezed through the noisy crowd and plunged beneath the stretch of red canvas. Storm sighed with relief as the worst of the sun heat was blocked.

"Wow," said Cloud. "And that's an understatement."

The tent was crammed with stalls. Performers and food sellers had set up shop everywhere.

"Bellum Town is amazing!" said Cloud. "I'd give my teeth to live here always. How does she do that without ripping her gullet?" He pointed to a woman swallowing long iron skewers. "Is it another sort of magic?"

"Don't know." Storm watched the skewer-eater but couldn't get Cloud's words out of her head. *Would* I *rather live here than Yanlin?* Now that she was away from Talon's guards, she found herself agreeing with Cloud. Bellum Town was the most exciting place in the world. How could she return to Yanlin after this?

They strolled deeper into the enormous tent, winding through the crowd. Every face was stained red by the sunlight filtering through the sun-scorched canvas.

"Over there!" Cloud pointed to their right. "Air-magic! You can watch another Air-witch in action." He grabbed her hand and tugged her towards the performer.

A man was standing on a shoulder-height platform, facing his audience. He had a begging bowl at his feet, half full of coins. He was thin and stooped, his grey topknot perfectly combed and tied; his hands, face and feet clean; his elegant tunic made of bright-blue silk. Storm stared at him, fascinated. Despite the bowl, he wasn't a beggar in any sense she recognised.

The witch had a row of brightly coloured paper whirligigs arranged beside him on his platform. Storm watched as a young girl pointed to a red toy. The man with her put a copper in the bowl and the witch picked the toy up and tossed it high into the air. Then he whipped out a bamboo flute and began to pipe. Storm felt the music pulse through her: Air-music!

As the witch played, the toy spun higher and higher, its four stiff arms catching the magicked wind. Storm stared, awed by the skill required to make such delicate, controlled magic. The flute seemed to concentrate the flow of magic, make it easier to direct. It had never occurred to her that she might be able to use a musical instrument to control her power. Longing tore through her. What must it be like to be so at one with the Elemental power?

She glanced at Cloud and saw a rapt expression on his face. She remembered that he had dreamed of becoming an Air-witch, but though he had been Chosen by the Albatross, Cloud had no magic.

Toy after toy was tossed into the air, dancing like coloured fireflies for a while until the witch sent each toy spinning into the hands of its new owner.

"He's raking it in!" breathed Cloud. "No wonder there's so many witches in town. A witch would live rich here!"

"So the councillors said," Storm replied drily.

"Not that you would…" Cloud frowned at her. "You

wouldn't, would you?"

She decided to tease him. "What would you do, Cloud? You just said you wanted to stay here forever!" Storm watched his expressions tumble and change as fast as the whirligigs.

"Uh…"

Fire shot into the air from somewhere a few paces ahead. Storm froze.

"A Fire-witch! This should be good." Cloud pushed eagerly through the crowd, towards the column of orange fire reaching towards the canvas rooftop. He didn't hear her shout of protest. The rest of the crowd seemed to want to see the Fire-witch too. Storm found herself carried forward after Cloud as inexorably as a swimmer caught in a riptide. She clapped her left hand over the gold cuff hiding the scar on her right wrist. Surely it was all right. It wouldn't be the Salamander's assassin, just a witch come to make some money, like all the others in town.

Walled by human bodies, Storm was pushed forward step by step. Cloud glanced back, grabbed her hand. "Careful we don't get separated in this crush!" he shouted over the tumult of voices. In the distance, the Fire-witch's audience cheered. The flow of bodies slowed. Cloud still held on to her as he pushed and shoved, dragging her with him.

"Stop! This is close enough!"

But he kept tugging. Only when they popped out into a small circle of space at the very front of the crowd did Cloud let go. He shouted in her ear: "We're lucky to get this close!"

In front of them was a chest-high platform constructed of bricks and stone. Children perched on their parents' shoulders. Men, women and children munched street food and swayed and rocked in place to the sound of the drum beaten rhythmically by a man seated below the platform.

The Fire-witch stood on the platform of bricks, a large open iron pot full of glowing, flickering coals on a stand beside her. She was thin and bony, long-faced with a wide mouth. She wore a long red silk tunic that reached nearly to her ankles. It was embroidered in gold with images of a salamander. Seeing it, Storm instinctively tried again to shrink away, but the crowd held her firm. She watched, mesmerised, as the Fire-witch fed the fire with a bundle of dried twigs, then dipped an iron flagon into the flames that shot up from the brazier.

The witch lifted the flagon to her lips and drank fire, and the crowd screamed in delight and horror.

Nauseated, Storm watched a red glow illuminate the skin and bone covering the woman's mouth. The fire-gleam flowed down the witch's throat and into her chest.

The witch put down the flagon with a flourish, opened her mouth and spewed forth fire. The children in the crowd screamed. The witch whirled round twice, then tossed a thin bamboo oval high into the air. She spat out a thin streak of flame that shot into the air – an arrow made of fire! The hairs on the back of Storm's neck rose as she saw the shaft of fire shoot skywards and strike the bamboo as it tilted mid-air and began to fall to earth. The oval burst into flames and fell on to the upturned faces of the crowd as snow-white ash.

The glow inside the Fire-witch faded. Again, the woman whirled round and round until the bottom of her tunic bellowed out in circle of flowing red. She spread her arms and her long fingers fluttered.

The witch spun to a stop, gathered another handful of twigs and flung them on the brazier. Flames shot into the air and divided into countless droplets, like raindrops of fire. The burning beads spun up out of the iron bowl into the air. They jumped on to the woman's arms, shoulders and head, until she had a line of dancing flames sitting on her from fingertip to fingertip. She reached out her arms wide and – with a shriek of exultation – began to spin faster. The fire drops grew long, stretched thin, and twisted together until the woman and the flames she carried became one bending, twisting column of fire.

The crowd bellowed with rapture and horror. Bile rose in Storm's throat. Her heart hammered in her chest. She made herself look away from the platform and the human column of fire. And found herself gazing into the face of an old man who stood on the other side of the platform. White hair sprouted from his head, seeming to protest at being tidied into a topknot. He had a round, wrinkled orange face, like a persimmon. His nose was wide and flat, and his eyes nearly as large as those of the cling-monkey that sat on his shoulders.

She had found him!

As the old man looked into her eyes, the smell of ash and charcoal was swept away by the cool fragrance of the high jungles. For a five-breath, it felt like she was once more standing on Yanlin Mountain, looking out to the sea rolling on to the harbour beach.

The cling-monkey began to jump up and down.

Even over the crowd's applause she heard its shriek of alarm.

Storm heard the voice of the Tortoise in her head: *Beware the fire within and without!*

Her eyes jerked back to the performance. The woman had stopped spinning; the flames dwindled, separated. The Fire-witch stood, arms aloft, a hundred tiny red drops dancing in her hair, her clothes, her hands. The flames began to flicker. One by one, they went out.

The air itself felt queasy.

Storm looked for the old man. He and the monkey had disappeared. She didn't try to fight the panic: it was too strong. She twisted round, tried to push through the wall of bodies, failed. Storm turned back to face the witch, her heart thudding faster than the drum's beat.

The drummer bashed out a crashing crescendo that made the subsequent silence shocking. "Show your appreciation!" he cried, casting down his drumstick and picking up a large bowl, which he held out to the nearest members of the audience. Coins showered into the bowl. Cloud threw a handful of coppers, hollering at the top of his voice. People stamped their feet and called out to the Fire-witch, who began a series of regal bows.

Straightening from a bow, the witch glanced around the crowd. Her eyes skimmed over Storm, blinked, returned. The Fire-witch's gaze locked on to Storm and her face darkened with a look of pure enmity. Death danced in the woman's eyes.

Storm lurched backwards, trying once more to find a way through the human wall, once more failing. She watched in horror as the witch whirled to the brazier, grabbed up red-hot coals...

The air quivered, stank. There was a deep groaning, cracking sound, and the ground shifted beneath Storm's feet. She felt sudden, too-familiar nausea. Earthquake!

People around her screamed and began to shove. The old man with the monkey was suddenly standing in front of her, pushing her backwards into a space that hadn't been there a heartbeat ago. "Run!" he commanded.

She stood frozen and stared at him, thinking that his voice was remarkably youthful for such an old man. Screams filled her ears. She smelled something burning. The ground shook.

The monkey leapt from the old man's shoulders on to hers and clung to her, holding her around the neck. The warmth of its breath, the feel of its body shivering in terror, released her.

There was just space enough to turn round and stagger away from the stage, the fire, the terrified people. Somewhere in the crowd behind her she heard Cloud shouting her name. The old man grabbed her hand and tugged her away, into the winding maze of streets that was Bellum Town. Still, she held on to Thorn's boat.

14

Storm's legs wobbled, and she stumbled to a halt. The monkey clinging tightly to her neck scolded as she swayed, unsteady on her feet.

Balance!

"Did you speak?" She stared at the old man in wonder, remembering a different speaker, place and time.

"I said, can you walk a bit further?"

"Yes." The dizzy spell was passing. "And thank you. You saved my life."

"Not I, the Tortoise. We must keep going. We are not safe yet."

The Tortoise! It had condemned her mother to death. How could she trust the spirit ever again? But her terror of the Salamander left her little choice. The

Fire-witch would follow, would not rest until she was dead.

The old man smiled with a warmth that made the knot of fear in Storm's chest loosen, a bit. The cling-monkey muttered in Storm's ear as she followed her rescuer into an unknown part of town.

The brick-paved street became a dirt path. The last house came and went and still they walked on, following a high wall covered in peeling plaster. The old man paused beside a tangle of vines cascading down the wall, and Storm saw a small door, half hidden beneath the foliage. Her rescuer pushed the door open, took her hand and led her into a shady garden.

Vines twisted up trees and shrubs to form a green tent over her head. Storm breathed in the scent of honeysuckle and orange blossom. Unseen birds warbled. Bees muttered. Butterflies and dragon flies swooped and darted.

Sensing a presence, Storm looked up into the wistful eyes of a three-toed sloth, hanging motionless from a tree branch just above her head. It seemed to be smiling ... but then, sloths always looked like they were smiling. Beside it, the heavy coils of a snake looped over the same branch. The creature's flat head pointed at her, bead-eyes watching, tongue tasting the air.

"Tortoise?"

I am here.

A confusion of feelings bruised her mind. The Earth spirit had just saved her life. But…

"You let Dain die!" Storm wondered at her bravery. How dare she rebuke an Elemental spirit?

When the ancient voice spoke again it was as unhurried as ever: *I mourn with you. Dain was one of my most beloved Children. But if you had not saved Nim, Death would have come to Yanlin with monstrous force. A great catastrophe threatens, not just for Yanlin, but for every creature of the earth, sea or air.*

A sickly chill settled in Storm's belly.

Remember the tale your father told you – the story of how life was created. Fire was begat by the sun. It cares nothing for Life.

"What does the Fire spirit want? Why is it trying to kill me?"

She waited, but the voice was silent. When she looked up again, the sloth and snake had vanished.

"I hate riddles!" Storm muttered.

"I will ask you none, then," said the old man, "but I cannot vouch for Scoundrel, who is a very disobedient soul."

The cling-monkey gave a chittering cry and leapt

up to disappear into the maze of vines and branches overhead.

"Touchy!" commented the old man.

Storm gazed after the monkey, missing the warm weight of the creature on her shoulder. She asked the old man, "Why have you brought me here?"

"To give you some refreshment. You have had a shock." He beamed at her. "And because you are the Weather-witch of Yanlin. More, you are the Child of Three Elementals, for the Tortoise claims you also."

Storm felt the hairs on her arms lift and shivered. No one knew that. No one but the Elders of Yanlin and her cousin Minnow.

"The Tortoise told me."

Of course: he was an Earth-witch. She watched him shuffle off towards a wooden hut just visible through the tree branches and wished the monkey would return. Slowly, she followed the old man.

"Seat yourself!" He pointed to the mats scattered on the porch and Storm sank down on one, carefully placing her parcel beside her. She felt the toy boat through the wrapping, amazed to find that the old woman's creation had survived intact.

The Earth-witch bustled about the tiny yard in front

of the hut. He plucked up a simple unglazed teapot from where it sat on top of a sunbaked stone and poured something into two cups. He put the cups on a tray and carried it into the back of the hut. Storm listened to him opening cupboards, clattering about, and realised that, for the first time since arriving on Bellum Island, she felt safe. If she listened long enough, perhaps the Fire-witch trying to kill her would become just a story she had made up to scare herself.

Her rescuer brought the tray back to the porch and placed it on a mat. Then he lowered himself to sit beside her, with a creaking of joints that reminded her, wistfully, of Teanu.

"Eat! Drink!" he ordered. "You will feel better afterwards."

The tray held a plate of tiny flat cakes along with the cups of amber liquid. She lifted the nearest cup. The contents looked and smelled like tea, but she had not seen him boil water. The old man took up a cup and slurped loudly.

Storm took a tentative sip. "Delicious, thank you! But how did you brew tea without hot water?"

"With the heat of the sun and enough time. I do not suffer Fire to enter my garden, which is why you are safe here."

"You have no cook fire?"

"I eat fruit, nuts, vegetables and seeds. These biscuits, for example, are sun-dried."

"No rice?" Storm stared at the old man in horror.

"Friends bring me steamed rice from time to time." The old man grinned at her. "When I get the craving. Now, eat! We have not much time."

"Time for what?"

"We have not met by accident, Storm. The Tortoise asked me to watch over you while you are on Bellum Island. You are in great danger. The Salamander grows impatient for your death."

Storm's throat dried, and her mouthful of biscuit turned into a choking-dry lump. Cheeks bulging like a squirrel, she sieved tea into her mouth until she could swallow. And still choked. When Storm had finished coughing, she asked, "*Why?* Do you know why?"

"Why do you think?"

"The Balance?"

He nodded. "The Tortoise confirms it."

"But what has the Balance to do with me?"

"Everything." He gazed at her, his eyes dark with worry. "With you, with the Pact, with the Drowned Ones. Bellum Island is the focus of the Salamander's ambitions. The danger lies here. The people of Bellum have been exploited by those whose ancestors grabbed power—"

"You mean the Fifteen Families. Yes, there is something wrong here ... the way the townsfolk look at members of the Pact." She shivered. "And there is poverty that our Elders would not permit. I have seen children stealing! Dirty, hungry-looking children. How can such a rich island let its children starve?" She watched the old man, hoping he would explain, but his face was impassive. "My uncle told me Bellumers have stopped making."

"It is all true. The Fifteen grabbed power generations ago. They live only to consume, caring nothing for others. As a result, this island is about to descend into civil war. You must stop that happening."

"Me?" Storm stared, appalled. "How can I stop a war?"

"You will have to find the answer to that riddle. You must be able to stop the conflict. That is why you were Chosen by Three." He took a slurruping sip of tea with obvious relish, then said, "Do not look to the power of magic. You were granted magic to keep you alive, but the source of magic is the Elemental that granted it, not the human child who wields it. Magic can be taken back as easily as it was given. Your talents lie elsewhere."

Talents? Storm knew she had no talents, other than story-telling. The goldsmith had promised that this man would help her, but he was just confusing her. She was more scared than ever. "I told you, I'm no good at riddles!"

"I hope very much that you are wrong." He smiled. "Now you must go back to Talon's house. We will meet again soon. Study the Pact. Find a solution," said the old Earth-witch.

"How do the Drowned Ones come into this?"

He gazed at her, his expression patient. "A clever predator attacks when its prey is weakest."

Her face grew warm. It seemed so obvious.

"Now it is time for you to go. It would be most unfortunate if the Pact found you here. I am too old to enjoy the prospect of playing hide-and-seek with their guards." He got to his feet, with a renewed popping and creaking of old bones.

"Wait!" Storm cried. "Tell me, is there an active rebellion? Should I contact them? How do I find them?" But the old man shuffled away as if she had not spoken. The monkey appeared, scampered after the Earth-witch and climbed him as if he was a tree, settling on one shoulder.

Storm shoved the last of her biscuit in her mouth and followed. Instead of answering her questions, the old man peppered her with instructions as he led her towards the door in the wall.

"Avoid Fire at all costs! The Salamander's witch is powerful. I have heard tell of her, and you would do well to stay out of her way. Do not travel the town alone! When you have news – anything, no matter how trivial you think it – send me a message. I may not be here, but Scoundrel will always find me, if you cannot."

"Scoundrel?" Storm blinked in surprise. The cling-monkey was muttering mutinously under its breath and tugging at the old man's beard.

"Scoundrel will stay with you. If you have a message for me, tell it to the creature. He is far cleverer than he looks! And now, you must go."

15

The Pact's guards caught up with Storm in a quiet residential street not far from the main square. "Mistress Storm, how nice to see you again." Tolbar wasn't smiling. She spotted Scoundrel and her not-smile became a glare. "What..." The guard pointed to the monkey, who had gone very still, "...is *that*?"

"Scoundrel. He's mine."

"It probably has vermin! You cannot take him back to the Master's house!"

"Then, unfortunately, I will have to return to my uncle's ship." Storm gave the guard a chilly smile. "Give my apologies to Talon, won't you?"

Tolbar drew a deep breath. They looked at each other with complete understanding. "Huh. Bring the creature if you must!" The woman motioned for her companions to form a phalanx around Storm. Tolbar scolded her all the way back.

The guard would doubtless be reprimanded over today's adventures. Storm felt guilty until the moment Tolbar ushered her into the guardhouse and she saw Cloud standing in a corner with his hands tied behind his back and a bruise on his left cheek.

"What have you done to him?"

"We've done nothing to him other than arrest him."

"He's hurt!"

"I got knocked down in the panic." Cloud actually grinned. He was enjoying the whole thing! *Why didn't the Elementals Choose him?* asked Storm's mind-voice. *He'd probably love having a Fire-witch trying to kill him!*

"Untie him. He's my friend."

"So he says." Tolbar made no move to release Cloud, who was watching the proceedings with wide-eyed interest. "The boy is a witness and a possible suspect."

Storm realised she was being punished for running off. "Suspect? What are you talking about?"

"What do you know about the incidents in the market tent earlier today?"

"Nothing."

"I find that hard to believe. Is she telling the truth, boy?" Tolbar took a menacing step towards Cloud. He darted a glance at Storm, then shrugged.

"Are you calling me a liar?" Storm challenged the guard.

Tolbar turned away from Cloud and stood with her hands on her hips, eyes narrowed.

She's afraid of me, Storm thought. *And also afraid of offending me.* Storm almost felt sorry for the woman – who had certainly not had a good day.

"Other witnesses report that the Fire-witch attacked the crowd where you and this boy were standing."

"Did anyone get hurt?"

Tolbar shrugged. "A few minor injuries. Fortunate that the mini-quake happened. It scared the witch off, it seems. We're looking for her."

"I don't know anything about it, and Cloud certainly doesn't, so you can let him go back to his ship. My uncle will be wondering where he is." Still the guard made no move to untie her shipmate. Storm took a gamble: "Let him go or fetch Talon! Does your master know you've detained my friend? Shall I ask him?"

Tolbar scowled. Storm could see what giving in cost her. "Untie the boy," she barked at her companion.

Once untied, Cloud rubbed his wrists, eyes wary. His face was carefully impassive as he turned to Tolbar. "Am I free to go?"

"Go on. Get out! And stay out of trouble in future."

Cloud's only reply was a polite bow. Then, with a wink at Storm, he strode from the room. Storm heaved a sigh of relief as he disappeared. Cloud had said nothing about the Fire-witch. Maybe he hadn't noticed whom she was trying to kill.

<hr>

Storm put her precious grave gift and wire monkey on the table before collapsing on to her bed. Dinner was brought to her room on a tray. Tolbar had had plenty of time to make her report, which would not have been friendly.

There was no food for Scoundrel so Storm shared bits of her supper. She showed him the soil bucket and hoped he was as intelligent as his master had claimed. Then, too tired even to attempt to draw the events of the day in her journal, Storm drifted off into uneasy dreams of hidden gardens and women dancing in columns of fire. She tossed and turned for a long time, unable to get comfortable on the too-soft mattress. Finally, she fell into a sound sleep.

<hr>

Shrick-gna-umm-shrick-ggrawm. The sound of gnawing and nibbling pulled Storm from fitful dreams. A rat must have crawled up from the hold of the *Wayfarer* and was eating her chalk and chewing the oiled leather of her journal! Light pressed against her eyelids, swaying with the motion of the ship.

Storm opened her eyes and didn't know if she was glad or sorry to find she was still in Talon's house. The trees in the garden were being lashed by an easterly. The leafy arms of the willow outside her window waved to and fro in front of the window, casting shadows on the ceiling. Still something gnawed.

Storm pushed herself up in bed. Betaan sat on the floor a few paces away. Talon's daughter reached a casual hand to the tray beside her, picked up a fat hazel nut and gave it to Scoundrel. She stroked his silky fur with her free hand. The cling-monkey sat in Betaan's lap, gnawing greedily.

Traitor! thought Storm.

"How did you acquire this little scamp?" Betaan's fingers caressed. Scoundrel chewed, his eyes darting from the tray of biscuits and nuts to Storm's face and back. "He's adorable!" trilled Talon's daughter. There was no mistaking the light of battle flickering in her eyes.

Punishment for yesterday's escape was about to be delivered. The monkey wrinkled his nose at Storm, showing his teeth in a cheeky grin. The Earth-witch's messenger was enjoying the situation far too much.

"That flea-bitten little rogue?"

Scoundrel squeaked in outrage. His expression made Storm want to laugh.

"I bought him from a horrible man who was making him perform tricks. He was beating the animal."

"Aren't you the virtuous one! But in Bellum Town there are hundreds of animals – and humans, for that matter – forced to do unsavoury work. You can't save them all, you know."

"But you could. The Pact runs the island. Why don't they do something about it?"

The other girl's eyes widened in surprise. "It isn't our responsibility to tell people how to live. The Pact was created to support trade and to make a profit for our families."

"You're talking about your own people! Bellum Islanders."

A look of revulsion crossed Betaan's face. "My people are the Pact. A flea-ridden thief is nothing to do with me!" She gave a sharp laugh, dismissing the subject. "I just hope you were joking and *this* little fellow is free of vermin."

Scoundrel sat still, watching Storm.

"Where did you get the money to pay for him?"

asked Betaan, far too casually.

Storm saw the trap. That smooth, doll-like face hid a mind as sharp and devious as her father's. "A shipmate loaned me some money."

"How very generous! Cling-monkeys are ridiculously fashionable. A young one like this costs much silver, especially in such prime condition. Those beatings must have been gentle, for he hasn't got a mark on him." She smiled, point scored.

"Yes," said Storm. "Isn't it lucky?"

Betaan changed tack. "Mer and I were *very* worried!" Her large, kohl-lined eyes took on an injured expression.

"How unfortunate." Storm's own expression grew deeply sorrowful. "I got separated from the guard on the way to the latrine."

Betaan's eyebrows rose in a disbelieving arch. "Tolbar says you ran from her. Like a dirty little thief." The last three words were spaced for emphasis.

Storm's eyes narrowed. Betaan, she realised, didn't much like her. She was vaguely surprised to find she didn't care.

"Is Tolbar a liar?" asked Talon's daughter.

Storm shrugged, attempting the world-weariness Betaan often cultivated. "I wanted to explore – on my own – without being constantly followed by guards. I suppose I should apologise."

"You must never do it again!" Betaan pushed the monkey from her lap and rose to her feet. Scoundrel leapt up a bedpost and perched on top. Talon's daughter held the tray out to Storm. "Here. I've brought you breakfast."

"That's kind of you." Storm gave the other girl a genuine smile and took a biscuit. She was very hungry. The crunchy pastry tasted of nuts and cinnamon. She ate, and Betaan continued to scold: "Father was very upset indeed. I don't like seeing him so distressed. It *was* unkind, after all we have done for you!"

Storm nodded, her mouth too full for speech.

"You must promise me never again to go into town without the guards!"

Storm popped the rest of the biscuit in her mouth and chewed slowly, choosing her words with care. "While I remain your guest, I will do everything I can not to worry you or your father. And do ask Mer to forgive me."

"Mer will forgive you, of course." Betaan had been successfully distracted. "But you cannot imagine her distress! At first, she thought you'd been taken ill. You must know, Mer dotes on you. And then, when the guard returned to say that you'd run off, she was convinced that you had been kidnapped and was distracted with worry!"

"I'm sorry." Storm meant it this time. She doubted Mer had become ill over her, but she had never had a girl friend. Still, unless she stayed on Bellum Island, the possible friendship could never be more than a glimpse of something that might have been.

16

That evening Talon held a formal dinner. Storm sat opposite her host. Betaan sat beside her and kept up a stream of amusing chat in her right ear. The other guests were robed in dragonfly green, rich purple, melting amber. Painted faces smiled on every side; the air was heavy with perfume. Storm felt like she had wandered into a gathering of glittering ghosts.

Storm laughed obediently at one of Betaan's jokes, doing her best to imitate Mer, sitting opposite, who always managed to look amused yet somehow apart.

Talon smiled, painted eyebrows forming perfect hoops. He rang the silver bell that sat on the table in front of him. At once, servants appeared to whisk away platters of uneaten food and refill cups with tamarind brandy.

"Let us drink to our most honoured guest, friends!" called Talon. "Join us, Storm. We drink to you!" He lifted his cup.

Mer drank, then smiled warmly at her. The Pact leader drained his cup and deposited it on the table, fingers stroking the thin porcelain. Storm thought of the bowl her mother had made for her Choosing gift. It was simpler, less showy, but she preferred it to anything here.

Talon leaned towards her. "I have an offer to make you, Mistress, one which will be of great benefit to both of us. Ladies and gentlemen! Attend me!"

Every eye in the room fastened upon them.

"Mistress Storm," Talon said in the same official voice. "You are a powerful Weather-witch. The Pact is always on the lookout for opportunity, and we see ways to harness your magic to our mutual benefit. Therefore, we have gathered tonight to offer you a rare – nay, a singular – opportunity." He paused, glancing around the room.

Talon was making his bid to win her from Yanlin. How could she turn this situation into a means of preventing civil war on the island and stop the Salamander breaking the Balance? The task felt impossible!

Her host waited, but when she said nothing he raised one eyebrow and continued. "As you may know, the Fifteen – the original families – have controlled world trade for countless generations. Never before, in the illustrious history of the Pact, has the opportunity I am about to offer you been granted to an outsider!"

He paused again to watch the effect of his words, but Storm kept her face carefully blank.

"We offer you the chance to become one of us! Full membership in the Pact, for you and your descendants, forever! You will also," Talon added in a smugly confident voice, "be allowed to *have* descendants! You would live with us as a girl and woman, not a non-sex. In time, we will find you a suitable life partner." His eyes flicked to someone in the watching group. Involuntarily, Storm glanced in the same direction.

Almond stood between Mer and Betaan, his arms crossed, an amused expression on his face. But beneath the practised sophistication, Storm saw a need for more power, more wealth – more of everything. So that was it. She repressed a shiver of revulsion. Of course, there were other men and boys on Bellum. Perhaps someone who was kind and funny, like Thorn, although, glancing around the room, she saw little evidence of kindness in the painted faces.

Talon had targeted her weak spot. She still mourned the family she could never have. But family meant Ma and Minnow, and her memories of Da. It meant Elders like Teanu. Storm remembered the ragged girl who had been caught thieving. Family meant something different here.

"You do not speak." Talon's voice was still confident.

Sweat gathered in her armpits, turning them prickly. She saw Mer gazing at her across the table. The other girl's eyes were fierce with anxiety. Storm felt a surge of gratitude: Mer was worried for her!

"I await your reply." Patience was ebbing from Talon's voice.

"My apology. Your generosity stunned me into silence."

"And does our offer interest you?"

"How could it not interest me? But I cannot make such an important decision without knowing what you want in return. I do not think it is merely the pleasure of my company at dinner."

Talon's smile widened. Chuckles of approval circled the room. This was the language they understood. Verbal fencing, bargaining!

"Your presence is a charming addition to our gatherings, of course, but yes. We would expect you to be our Weather-witch and use your magic as we direct."

"But you don't have a trading fleet." Storm stated the obvious. "And your harbour is impervious to attack. Why does Bellum need a Weather-witch?"

"Defence is never to be taken lightly. Even with the lava wall, we can use a powerful witch. Call it insurance."

Storm just stopped herself rubbing her nose in frustration. "Pretty expensive insurance. What else?"

"There might be other jobs. But those can be discussed as they arise. No need to bother you with details now. Basically, we would expect you to fight for us against enemies of the Pact."

"Can you be a bit more specific?" Storm asked. "'Enemies of the Pact' is a pretty flexible description. Who would I have to fight?"

He shrugged, too casually. "Anyone who threatens us. Like the Drowned Ones, for instance. Their rafts have been spotted in the Inner Sea for the first time in living memory. Or … others."

Storm's heart lurched. If the old Earth-witch was right – if the Drowned Ones were already here – then civil war must be imminent. But how would the pirates know that? She thought of Nim, and hatred flared afresh. The Drowned Ones were no strangers to using spies.

"What 'others'? I won't agree to anything until I know what I'm up against."

Grudging respect flared in Talon's eyes. "You're right, of course. But you needn't worry. We simply want a hand dealing with a bit of domestic unrest."

"And why do you need me? I am a Weather-witch, not a town guard!"

"We have been gathering up troublemakers and n'er-do-wells. Thieves, of course. But also malcontents who stir up unrest. Scum from the lowest dregs of society. In our mercy, we have no wish to execute them. Exile is not ... practical. That leaves imprisonment."

Cold fingers brushed her spine as she remembered the woman who had given her the knife. *Execute?* He had said the word so casually – as though killing his fellow islanders was a perfectly acceptable course of action.

Talon hadn't noticed her shock. "We have commissioned a brace of cargo hulks – sturdy, capacious ships. We intend to keep the traitors on these ships."

"For how long?"

"Until they die, of course. It is exile, but safer, you see."

Safer for the Fifteen Families, he meant. There must be so many rebels that he feared those who survived exile to sea might find each other and form a second resistance – one that might gain sufficient numbers and strength and return to their island to fight. Might even collaborate with…

"The Drowned Ones!" she hissed under her breath. Was someone in the rebel group collaborating with the pirates? But that was unthinkable…

"What did you say?"

"Nothing! Only … I still don't see why you need me."

"Merely to keep the prison ships safe and … isolated. If the need arose, which is very unlikely, of course."

Isolated from the Drowned Ones. Storm saw Mer looking at her, jaw clenched with anxiety, and felt suddenly sick. The Pact were tyrants, each and every one of them, and they wanted her to help them stay in power. Crushing the rebellion would avert a civil war, but there must be another way – the Tortoise, the old man, they could not have meant this!

And there was a more pressing problem. What would Talon and his Fifteen Families do when she declined their offer? Looking at the greed in the faces of the men and women surrounding her, Storm thought their reaction might not be entirely hospitable, and for the first time that night, she was afraid.

Water could not aid her here, and she had faint hope of raising much of a wind inside this room. She was trapped, and totally on her own.

17

"We await your answer." Talon's eyes burned with barely controlled frustration. Outside the closed door, if she guessed correctly, waited dozens of armed guards, including archers. If she said no to the Pact's proposal, Talon might well try other means of persuasion, like keeping her prisoner until she agreed to his plans. And what if he realised her sympathy was with the rebels?

It occurred to her that Talon had gambled hugely in disclosing his plans to her. After all, an overthrow of the Pact might suit all the other islands, including Yanlin, who might broker better deals with the rebels.

Storm's nose itched with frustration; she clenched her fists to keep from rubbing it. The Albatross and Dolphin were powerless to help her here. What about the Tortoise? The Earth spirit? Elementals did not come when called, only when they chose. Besides, it would be best to outwit Talon. If she could…

"You cannot expect me to have an answer at my fingertips, just like that! It's a big decision. I need time to think it over."

It wasn't the answer he wanted. His nostrils flapped as he took in a calming breath. "What is there to think over? Your life will be better with us than back on Yanlin. We offer power, wealth and the right to live as a female. We offer you a future family. Children! Can your old island offer so much?"

"Indeed not. You offer me more than I dared hope for."

"Then what is there to think over?" Talon's brows were a thick, flat line. No hoops of smugness to be seen.

"I cannot consider myself only."

"Who else? Your uncle? I understood most of your family is dead. Or do you still hold some quaint ideas about loyalty to your Elders and the island?"

"Not at all," Storm said, as calmly as she could. "But I answer to the Elemental spirits who granted me magic. The Albatross and Dolphin have plans for me. I am sure you have no wish to offend the Elementals."

"Offend the…" Talon stared at her blankly, his face chalky beneath the layer of paint. The assembled guests muttered. Betaan's black-rimmed eyes popped wide. None of them had thought about the beings who had bestowed her with magic, just what her power could do for them.

"Do you think magic is given with no strings attached?" Storm asked.

"But…" Talon was almost stammering. "Surely it could make no difference to the spirits! Other witches change allegiance from island to island all the time."

"If I was like other witches I wouldn't be here."

Talon's eyes narrowed as he peered at her, trying to read her intentions. Everything hinged on this moment.

"You want me for a friend." Storm was amazed at how calm her voice sounded. "I want that too. You wouldn't like me as an enemy – ask the Drowned Ones. And I don't think you want the Albatross and Dolphin as your enemies either. Or the Tortoise, of course," she added thoughtfully.

Her opponent licked his lips. Sweat beaded on his forehead, trickled down, marring his face paint. "Can you ask the Elementals if they object to your change of allegiance?"

"I can try," Storm lied solemnly. "But it will take time."

"If you gain their assent, you will agree to our terms?"

"The Pact's generosity is overwhelming. I am deeply honoured!" Storm hoped her words would be taken as assent. Her heart thudded; had she won herself time?

All around the room, expressions of smugness had been replaced with frowns of doubt and worry. Mer's face wore a look of bitter disappointment. So ... there had never been any real hope of friendship there – it had all been about wealth and power. Storm felt nauseous. She longed to be away from here, out of this too-warm room with its stink of rich food and perfumes, away from the flickering oil lamps and greedy faces.

"You have one day." Talon tapped his long red nails together. "By the end of tomorrow we will expect you to have reconciled the Elemental spirits to our plan."

"I need a five-day at least!"

"One day!" Clack-clack-clack went the scarlet claws.

Storm bowed. Before tomorrow evening, she would escape this house, find Uncle Lake and sail away from Bellum Island, out of the Pact's reach!

Now that she knew Talon's plans for prison-ships, she didn't think anything could stop the coming rebellion. The only way to prevent the Drowned Ones from attacking Bellum if war came was to go to sea and hunt them down herself. Cloud was right: it was time she finished the job she had failed to do in Yanlin Harbour.

This time, she would destroy the enemy!

"I shall go at once," she said, "and try to contact the Elementals."

———→

She was thinking so hard that she didn't notice Mer follow her up the stairs until Storm had opened the door to her bedroom. The older girl pushed past into the room. It was so unlike the cool, amused Mer that Storm stood and stared. Mer pulled her inside and closed the door.

"May I come in?"

"You are in."

"I wanted a quick word. Do you mind?"

Storm shrugged, wanting Mer to leave so she could be alone to think.

"You look ill," said Mer. "Are you all right?"

"Fine." Storm went into the bathing room and rinsed her face in the lacquered basin, which always seemed to be freshly filled. She stared down into the bowl, watching drops of red and yellow face paint stain the water.

"Did you enjoy the dinner?" Mer stood in the doorway.

"Not much."

"You do realise that guards were waiting outside the

dining room for your answer? Talon would have used force to 'persuade' you." Mer's voice was expressionless.

Storm felt her heart began to beat faster. Why tell her this? She laid the towel carefully beside the basin, turned to confront the older girl. Mer's hands were shaking.

When the truth occurred to her, it was so unexpected it made Storm dizzy. "You're not upset because I haven't agreed to Talon's offer. You're upset because I might!"

Mer watched her warily, as if trying to decide something. At last she said, "You're only guessing! Even if you're right, why should I trust you? You might have already decided to work for *them*!"

"But you're one of 'them'." Except it was obvious that Mer wasn't. She was seeing the real Mer for the first time – and this stranger was full of anger, even hatred. Hatred of the Pact and anyone who might help them. But why?

Mer frowned. Storm could see her mind whirring. At last the older girl said, in a low voice, "We cannot talk in this house. There are eager ears everywhere. That brat could burst in here at any moment. She despises you, you know. Calls you 'The Bumpkin'. She's jealous, of course. She wants Almond for her consort when

Talon is dead and she's running things!"

Storm already knew Betaan's true feelings, and right now they didn't matter. This was her chance! "I have no intention of helping the Pact. I had to stall for time. You're right – we can't talk here. Help me get out of this house unseen, and you can tell me why you hate them so much."

Mer watched her through narrowed eyes. At last she nodded. "I must go. Talon's servants count people in and out of this house. Expect me after moonrise."

"Expect you where?"

"Just be ready!" With a last, calculating glance, Mer stalked from the room. Storm listened to the soft thud of her bedroom door closing and wondered what had just happened, and whether she was wise to trust the enigmatic Mer to lead her into the night and the unknown danger that was almost certainly waiting there.

18

Storm sat cross-legged on her bed in the dark time between sunset and moonrise, listening to Scoundrel pad back and forth across the floor. The cling-monkey was muttering under his breath. After Mer had left, he had leapt on to her shoulder and began to scold, with much moaning and chittering of teeth. Scoundrel had even pulled her hair for emphasis until she gently set him on the ground.

"No point in being cross with me! I have to escape tonight and Mer is my best chance."

The cling-monkey snorted derisively. Storm decided to ignore him: she was nervous enough already. And what did a monkey know, after all?

The wait in darkness seemed endless, but at last a cool light silvered the window, waxing stronger until

Scoundrel's shadow followed him as he paced back and forth across the room.

Storm clapped her hand over her mouth, stifling a cry. Mer loomed over her, her face merely two glinting eyes in the dimness. She had let herself into the room without making any noise.

"Follow me." The whispered words were a command. Mouth dry, Storm rose to her feet, gesturing for Scoundrel to follow. The monkey showed his teeth in a ferocious grimace, but obeyed.

Mer led her through long, confusing corridors, up winding stairs and out a narrow attic window on to a rickety wooden parapet at the top of the house.

Holding tightly to the slender railing, Storm looked down at the moonlit shapes of the trees in the garden far below and wished herself safely back in her bed. She might be an Air-witch, but she didn't have wings, and she was quite certain that she could not fly!

Something leapt on to Storm's shoulder and wound both long furry arms around her throat. "Careful, Scoundrel!" Storm held her breath and waited for her heart to stop jumping like a frog in the rain. "A bit of warning next time, please!"

The cling-monkey chuntered in her ear. It sounded suspiciously like a giggle.

"Quiet!" Mer hissed. "We're near the servants' sleeping quarters. Hurry – this way."

"Wait!" Storm put a hand on the other girl's arm, drew her near and said in a low voice, "Why have you brought me up here?"

"If you don't trust me, go back." Mer's eyes glittered in the moonlight.

Storm's heart was full of misgivings. How could she escape Talon's house from the attics? Was this some sort of complicated trick? Was Mer loyal to the Pact after all? Was she going to fling her off the roof? Storm gripped the hilt of her knife. Mer turned without another word and glided along the wooden parapet to the end of the house. Where she instantly disappeared.

Storm approached the spot where Mer had vanished, heart thudding. Had the girl fallen, or...? No! Now she could see that the platform continued around the side of the house where it became a wooden ladder descending into the shadows. Mer was already out of sight. Storm sighed and stepped gingerly on to the ladder. It was even more rickety than the parapet. Each step groaned as she put her weight on it.

"Hurry!" The single word floated up.

Scoundrel clinging tight, Storm climbed down and down and down. At last her foot touched solid ground.

This side of the house lay in blinding darkness. A hand grabbed her elbow, tugged.

And then they were creeping through the back garden, darting from tree to tree, keeping in the shadows. Past the carp pond and far into the garden. When they were out of sight of the house, Mer set off at a trot. Storm followed close on her heels. Scoundrel made huffing noises in her ear, as though urging her on. Within a few breaths, they were at the far end of the wall encircling the garden. It was the height of two men and made of lumps of stone mortared and made smooth with a facing of clay.

The older girl turned to face Storm. "There is a way here over the wall. Here!" And she pointed to a deep crack in the wall where the smoothed clay had crumbled away from the stones.

The holes would serve as hand- and footholds, Storm saw at once. She thought she could see signs of it having been used recently.

"Yes, I came this way. Now, follow me."

It was an easy climb. Easier than what faced them on the other side. Storm was glad of the moon's light as she stumbled and scuffed through tangled plants and rubble. Bamboo grew head-high but someone had beaten a winding path through its stems.

They had only travelled a few paces when Mer stopped. "We can talk here." They were in a small clearing, just large enough for two people to stand face to face. "Promise me!" said Mer without any preamble. "Promise that you won't ever work for Talon against the people!"

Storm winced: the other girl's passion was like a furnace blast. "Slow down! First, you tell me why you hate him so much. You're from the Fifteen. Your family is rich. Why do you care?"

"Have you seen the poverty on this island? The desperation of the people? You've been spending too much time with Betaan!" Mer's voice was scathing. "You have no idea how much it has cost me, pretending to be her friend. At least she's so self-obsessed that it was easy to trick her into thinking I actually like her. She expects everyone to fall at her feet in adoration!"

"All right," said Storm. "Maybe you aren't as selfish as Talon and his daughter, but you can't tell me this isn't personal. If you want me to trust you – to be open about my plans – tell me why you are working against your own kind."

Mer hesitated, eyes narrowed. Then she shrugged. "It *is* personal. They killed my father."

"Who did?"

"Talon and that unnatural demon, Waffa!"

"The tally-keeper?"

"My mother."

Storm rubbed her nose, hard, waiting for the shock to lessen. There was no physical resemblance between the sour-faced Waffa and graceful, tall Mer, but now that Mer was no longer acting a part Storm could see a similar ruthlessness in the daughter's eyes. "Your mother *murdered* your father?"

"She betrayed him to his death. For profit!" Mer's lip curled. "The Fifteen would eat their own children if there was enough profit in it. When I was small the old chief councillor died, and my father decided to compete with Talon for leadership of the Pact.

"He was an honourable man, my da. Which did not make him popular with the Fifteen. He saw that the ordinary people of Bellum were growing rebellious. Our island's makers were dying off and the Pact did not bother to organise apprenticeships for the newly Chosen. 'Why go to the bother?' they asked, 'when we get all the goods we need from other islands?' Even the fisher-folk were no longer going out with their nets. The Fifteen grew richer and richer while every year the people became poorer and more resentful. My father foresaw trouble and wanted to guide the Pact into a new path – one of sharing wealth and power."

Tears of rage armoured Mer's eyes behind a glassy shield. "My loving mother listened to his words, then repeated them to Talon. Da was accused of treason. He was set adrift in a tiny rowing boat with a five-day supply of water and no food. He is dead, his body lost forever! I shall not even meet him in the afterlife."

It was the nightmare that had haunted Storm since childhood: a raging sea, an overturned boat, the body of a man floating face down in the waves. "My father died at sea when I was five. But my chief Elder, Teanu, says that the soul still finds its way to the afterlife. She says that because this life is not fair, the next must be."

"But still you fear, don't you?" In the moonlight, Mer's face was a mask. Only her eyes lived, shine-full of hate.

"Yes."

"Well," said the older girl. "We share that at least. Now you have my story. I have been working with the rebels for years. We grow in strength every season. Soon, we shall destroy the Pact! And I shall myself put Talon and Waffa into a leaky boat and tow them out into treacherous waters!" She panted with the effort of hating. "Which is why I cannot allow you to help them."

Something in her voice made Storm's shoulders twitch. She took her time before saying, in a measured voice, "I would never help Talon. What he intends is evil."

"Even if it means you live as a non-sex for the rest of your life?" The eyes watched, unreadable.

"Even so." The older girl could surely do nothing to her: Storm had only to call the wind. But the sense of threat did not lessen.

"I believe you," said Mer at last. She placed both her hands on Storm's shoulders and pulled her into a brief, formal embrace. "I'm glad. I like you. I hoped, when I first met you, that we might become friends. But it would be best if you left Bellum Island. Go to your uncle's ship and leave my island tonight! For your own sake as well as ours."

"My sake?" Had Mer's eyes flickered? "Do you know something?"

"I know that Talon is devious and will not stop trying to convince or coerce you into working for him against us! You must leave."

"I think so too. But is there no other way except war?"

Mer drew herself tall. Her face grew austere, and the resemblance to Waffa was now striking. "It will be cleansing, not war. We will scour the evil from our land!"

"But many on both sides will die! Do you think their guards and soldiers will simply lay down their weapons and welcome you?"

Mer shrugged. "We will win."

"Can't your side negotiate with the Pact? The stakes are higher than you realise. The Elementals have told me that a war here could break the Balance!"

"The Balance!" Mer gave a soft laugh. "I had forgotten: you come from the edge of the world. The 'Balance' is a tale told to children, to make them behave."

"But the Unknowable One—"

"Does not exist! Or, if it does, it has travelled too far away to have anything to do with us now. The Pact is in charge because it took power, not because it deserves to rule! The only 'balance' is the one we make!"

"Does that apply even to the Drowned Ones?" Storm watched Mer's eyes for any flicker of guilt, any sign that she was in league with the enemy.

"You mean we should blame them for their own misfortune?" Mer gave a chilly smile. "It's a bit convenient to think that an island sinks because the people living on it are evil."

Storm sighed; Mer had given away nothing. "But surely you acknowledge that the Balance can be broken by the Elementals?"

Mer shrugged. "I told you, I don't believe in the 'Balance'. And as for the Elemental spirits, I am not sure they exist."

Storm stared. "Then where does magic come from?"

"Perhaps from inside witches themselves. Who knows? It doesn't matter."

Storm shook her head, shocked to her core. "Whose Child are you?"

Mer laughed again, as though Storm had said something very funny. "I did not undergo the ritual! No member of the Fifteen undertakes the Choosing. Why would we? We will never be apprentices. We rule, we do not make."

"But I have *seen* the Albatross, the Dolphin. The Tortoise speaks to me. The Salamander..." Her words dried on her lips. She would not confide about the Fire-witch to this girl full of hate.

Mer shrugged. "Perhaps you are right and I wrong. I don't know ... or care. But you must leave my island tonight. Promise!"

There was a fanatical glint in Mer's eyes. The threat in her voice was real. Yet Storm found there was still something about the other girl she liked. And it was moon-clear now that Weather-witch or no, she would never be able to influence the rebels. She could only save the Balance by hunting down the Drowned Ones and defeating them. Any civil war could be contained on this island. The Salamander would not win.

"I promise," said Storm. "I shall seek out my uncle and return to Yanlin."

Mer's face sagged with relief. "I am glad! Go, with my good wishes. This path leads to the harbour." After a last, considering look, the older girl turned on her heel and strode back the way they had come. The bamboo swallowed her with a shudder.

19

Storm pushed through the bamboo. The plants rattled and sighed, sounding as though a dozen hunters were stalking her through the grove. Her heart pounded, and she felt glad of Scoundrel's company.

At last she struggled through a particularly stubborn clump and found herself in a winding alley. Storm took careful note of where the tunnel began, breaking a stem and bending it down as a marker. Then, after a quick glance at the moon, which was already descending back towards its bed beneath the sea, she broke into a run. Time to find Uncle Lake and escape Bellum and the Pact.

The winding alley led to a street Storm recognised. *Thank the Ancestors!* This street led to the main road down to the harbour. Mer's route had bypassed the main square and its dangers.

Storm soon turned on to the harbour road, walking as quickly as she could. Even at this time of the night – approaching the dark time when the moon was swallowed by the sea – Bellum Town was not asleep. She had imagined that the streets would be empty, but lanterns still glowed outside taverns. Dark figures strolled through the night, intent on unknown business. Storm had dressed in her old ship-board clothes and tied her hair up in a topknot, and no one paid her any attention. She trotted down the harbour road and out on to the quay, looking for the *Wayfarer* among the tens of dozens of ships at anchor in the vast harbour.

Her eyes scoured the pennants, searching for the familiar flag of Yanlin, with its design of a seabird and quarter moon. It took many anxious breaths, many heartbeats squinting through the moonlight at the bobbing ships, listening to the familiar slosh of waves on wood, until Storm at last believed the evidence of her eyes. Yanlin's fleet was gone. The *Wayfarer* had sailed and left her behind!

She had not been so close to weeping since her mother's funeral. *You can't stay here!* warned her mind-voice. The town was patrolled night and day by the Pact's guards, and they would doubtless pay particular attention to the harbour warehouses. There was only one person who might be able to help.

"Let's go see your master, Scoundrel. Perhaps he will know of a way to contact Uncle Lake. I can't go back to Talon's house!"

"Huh!" The monkey grunted softly in her ear and, to her surprise, laid his cheek briefly against hers. Then he leapt to the ground and scampered further along the pier towards the headland. The creature stopped and looked back.

"No!" Storm hissed. "Not that way! Take me to your master's house. To the garden behind the wall!"

Scoundrel stayed where he was, waiting for her to follow, huge eyes shining in the fading moonlight. Storm remembered the old man's words: *He's cleverer than he seems.*

"Ancestors!" Storm muttered. But obeyed.

The cling-monkey led her past the pier and quay-side warehouses and along the strand until they reached the headland furthest from town. As she approached, Storm saw that a series of semicircular wooden doors lined the base of the cliff. They reminded her of the entrances to the shrines of the Elementals back on Yanlin. These doors must also open on to caves or rooms carved out of the rock, but if these caverns were shrines, the spirit being worshipped was that of Trade! They must be ancient warehouses. Most seemed to have fallen into disuse, the doors rotten and hanging off their hinges, showing gaping, toothless mouths.

Still Scoundrel scampered ahead, stopping regularly to see if she was following. He began to make anxious chittering noises, and she doubled her pace. The last of the caves neared. Above it sheer rock rose the height of many houses. *Halfway to the falling moon*, Storm thought. Surely the monkey wasn't going to ask her to climb that!

But Scoundrel paused in front of the disused warehouse. He chirruped encouragement and, with a swish of his long tail, disappeared into its open mouth.

"Come back!" Storm paused in the entrance. She could see rotting wood scattered about the rocky floor – all that remained of the door that had once protected the gathered treasures of the world's islands. But the slanting moonlight illuminated only a few paces of ground. And then … utter darkness.

"Scoundrel?" Her voice echoed around the invisible room, bouncing round and round. The chamber must be enormous. And then the monkey was back, scolding, bared teeth gleaming in the patch of moonlight. He reached up a long arm, grabbed her hand and tugged.

"All right," she said. "But don't you dare let go!"

The monkey led Storm under the earth. She walked for what seemed like an eternity, blinded by darkness. Her memory took her back to the night of her Choosing – the terrifying journeys into the shrines, alone in complete blackness.

This time a warm hand held hers tight. But for that, Storm knew, she would be running back towards the entrance. "Scoundrel?" she pleaded at last. "Are we nearly there?"

Somewhere ahead a light glimmered like a solitary star. Scoundrel gave a squeal of happiness and abandoned her. She heard the patter of his feet racing towards the light. Just as suddenly, her own fear disappeared.

I am here, Storm, said the Tortoise. Storm followed Scoundrel towards the light.

20

"Well done, my friend. Yes, you may have a cake. Now, do be quiet so we can hear ourselves think!"

An iron lantern stood on the damp stone floor of the tunnel. In its circle of light stood four people and one small orange monkey. The Earth-witch smiled at Storm in welcome as he placed a pack on the floor. Scoundrel grabbed it and scooped out a small cake. He settled down on his haunches, held the sweet to his mouth and began to nibble. The cling-monkey seemed to have forgotten Storm entirely.

She walked forward, studying the three strangers. There was an older man in a dark cloak. His hair and beard were streaked with grey and he looked strangely familiar. Beside him stood the young Water-witch she had met in town, and a smaller, frail-looking woman.

The three bowed in greeting. "We met in town," said the younger man.

Storm nodded. "I remember. You warned me about the Fire-witch. I saw you too," she said to the older man. "You are an Air-witch! I saw you in the red tent. I never thought of using a flute to focus magic. Will you teach me, Master—"

"I'm afraid we haven't time for lessons," interrupted the old Earth-witch. "Skill matters, Storm, but always remember that the Elementals control their magic. You can never master what does not belong to you. It is your other talents the Three seek to use."

"I have no other talents!"

It was true: other than storytelling, she had never had a talent for making. But the old man merely smiled in reply.

Three of the four gathered here to meet her were witches: Earth, Air, Water. Storm stared at the woman, unease making her heart beat harder.

"Yes." The woman spoke reluctantly, her words so faint Storm could barely hear them. "I belonged to Fire."

A gaunt woman dressed in crimson, flames shooting from her fingertips. Storm shuddered. "Why have you brought her here?" she demanded.

"She has relinquished Fire." The Earth-witch's voice was grave.

"Some of us have refused to do the Fire spirit's bidding, even at the price of our magic," the woman said. "I am a witch no longer."

"The Tortoise is here as a sign that you may trust us," said the Earth-witch. "The spirit told me you would come here. How else would we be waiting for you? We meet here, Under Earth, for your safety. Far from the island's old volcano. Here Earth is dominant. Nevertheless, we must hurry. The morning draws near and we have much to tell you. Please listen. The Tortoise itself asks this!"

"And the Albatross." The grey-haired man's eyes grew fierce, like those of a sea-eagle.

"And the Dolphin!" The young man smiled with joy.

The woman's eyes never left Storm's face. Now she said, "I do not speak for the Salamander. Only for those Fire-witches who fear that the spirit who claimed us as its human children will sacrifice everything – even the existence of life itself – for dominion over its old rival, Water!"

"But what can I do? What can any of us do?"

"You doubt yourself," said the Earth-witch. "You have run from Talon's house carrying hate in your heart, seeking the destruction of your enemy. You do not yet understand how important it is to prevent war – not just on Bellum Island, but war such as we have never known, where every hand is turned against its neighbour!"

"You mean the Drowned Ones? But they are our enemies!" Cloud's words echoed in her head. "It is our duty to avenge our dead!"

The old man did not reply.

"You have, I am told," said the Air-witch, "the makings of a Chanter. So you will know the old tales."

"I know some."

"Then you know that Fire was first sent into the World in order to destroy it. That it was prevented by being chained by Earth and imprisoned by Water."

"Yes. And the One admonished the Elementals to keep the Balance. How is it that Fire dares flout the will of the One?"

"Fire is impetuous and selfish," said the former Fire-witch. "It may believe the One will never return."

"All the Elementals are selfish." The Earth-witch spoke at last. "Even the Tortoise. They are not prone to introspection."

"Will the One return?" Storm asked.

"In its own time, which is not measured in human

years. Fire sought to destroy Water long ago. The tales speak of the time when the seas burned, and the mountains of the north-east islands woke in rage, erupted, burned and sank. Those that escaped the battle between sea and fire became the Drowned Ones."

"But it was their own fault that their islands sank! The homes of the Drowned Ones disappeared beneath the sea because the people who lived on them lacked virtue. Ever since, they have tried to steal our islands for themselves. The war between us is their fault!"

"It is important to remember who writes the tales," the old man said wryly.

"Humans are frail, even as the Elementals." He shrugged. "We fight because there is not enough land for all of us. But if life is to survive, we must find a new way."

"Know this," said the woman who had once been a Fire-witch. "The Salamander grows fat on hate. War makes it strong."

"But … how can we not hate those who hurt us?" Storm protested. "I saved the life of a Drowned One and then the boy betrayed me. My mother died because I trusted him!"

"Yes," said the old Earth-witch.

Storm wanted him to tell her that Dain's death

had been unavoidable. That it would have happened whether she had rescued Nim or not.

But the old man kept nodding. "Yes." Every word he spoke broke her heart anew. "Your mother died because you saved the boy. I am sorry."

"Do you desire the Drowned One's death?" asked the Air-witch. "Do you want vengeance?" The four adults waited. Even Scoundrel seemed to watch, his deep-set eyes strangely knowing.

"Yes."

"Yet I have told you the Salamander feeds on hate," said the woman who had been a Fire-witch. "You bear the proof on your right wrist."

It was true. Last year, her hatred of Mixi had made her vulnerable to the Fire Elemental. But this was different. "Nim betrayed me, pretended to be my friend! And all the time he was planning to help his people kill us and steal our island. My mother died because of his treachery. How can I not hate him?"

The Water-witch shrugged. "You are a Child of the Dolphin. The Trickster loves riddles. Try to use your talent with water to find a path."

Rebellion rose in her heart. "Why does it have to be me? Can't we do it together?"

"There will be a time for 'together'. That I do promise," said the Earth-witch. "But not yet. As for why you, why not? It must be someone. The Three chose you before you were born. Your job is to figure out what is special about you – what you are meant to do."

"You must be important or the Salamander would not be trying so hard to get rid of you," said the woman. "There is something about you that is a threat to its plans. Or perhaps it is something that will happen to you. Something you choose to do, or not to do."

"You must go now, Storm," said the Earth-witch. "Scoundrel will return with you."

The young man held something out to her. "Here, I want you to have this. The music is in you; just practise." He held out a small flute. "The smallest magic is always the hardest. But sometimes the most important."

She took the flute in a numb hand. Stared down at it, her fingers barely feeling the smoothness of the precious ebony. "Thank you. But cannot you teach me?"

"Everyone's music is different. Besides, there isn't time. The moon falls into the sea."

"But I can't go back to Talon's house! The Fifteen are trying to force me to work for them. They intend to cleanse the island of rebels. I went to the harbour to find my uncle and escape, but Yanlin's fleet has sailed. You must see that I can't go back!"

"You must!" The Earth-witch's expression was unyielding. "The Pact is the key to the battle to come. Bellum must not be allowed to descend into civil war. The Drowned Ones wait for the opportunities a war among the islanders will bring, and the Salamander desires a catastrophic war so it can feed on the hatred and grow ever stronger. You must try to influence the Fifteen."

"You don't know Talon."

The old man smiled. "I know more than you imagine. He is easily led by his desires. It is all part of the same riddle, Storm. You must also return to Talon's house tonight because the Pact offers you some safety from the Fire-witch. While you remain on Bellum they are your best hope of survival. I will try to find a way to contact your uncle. For now, you must stall Talon or trick him. And, most of all, stay alive!"

Your first duty is to survive. Go, child.

Storm bowed her head. She had no choice – she must choose to trust the Tortoise or lose everything she believed in, everything Dain had taught her, and become like Mer.

At a nod from his master, Scoundrel bounded forward and took her hand. The cling-monkey led her out from beneath the earth, towards danger.

21

The moon plunged into the sea as Storm climbed over the crumbling wall, and its light drowned with it. In blind darkness, she crept through the back garden of Talon's house, stumbling over tree roots, nearly falling into the carp pond.

At last her feet met paving stones, and the house rose above her, a towering presence almost invisible against the moonless sky. Storm edged in the direction she thought the wooden stairs to the attic must be, arms out, fingers searching. *Guide me, Ancestors!* she prayed. *Don't let me trip over something and wake the guards!*

Her fingers brushed wood, splintery and rough. She had found the steps. "Hold tight, Scoundrel!" The monkey seemed to be dozing. She too was longing for her bed. She would worry about Talon tomorrow; she still had most of the day to figure out how to outwit the Pact leader. She would talk to Mer again.

Storm began the climb. From somewhere behind her in the garden came a soft thudding noise. She froze. Was someone else out there? If it was one of the guards, they would raise the alarm and she would be in even more trouble. Talon was bound to guess that she had tried to escape to the *Wayfinder*. Did he have something to do with the disappearance of her uncle and the fleet?

Most certainly, replied her mind-voice. But we have other things to worry about!

Storm waited, breath caught in her chest, for more sounds she wasn't alone in the garden. Nothing. It must have been an animal. She steadied herself, began to climb, one cautious step at a time. Nearly at the top. She would soon be safely back in her room. Storm stepped on the next rung. As she did so, Scoundrel shrieked and jumped from her shoulders.

A sharp crack, a lurch, as the rung gave way beneath her foot.

The falling took forever and no time at all. She seemed to have too much time for thinking but no time for doing – no time for magic.

As she plummeted towards the earth, Storm knew

she would die. In a way, it was a comfort. She had failed, but at least she could stop now. Nothing would be her fault after this.

The ground rushed up to meet her. She could hear it coming. She squeezed her eyes shut and waited for stone and gravel to smash her bones to jelly. When she landed with a ridiculous-sounding squelch on something soft and springy, Storm gave a whimper of outrage. Shocked at being alive, she bounced two, three, four times, before quivering to a stop.

The ground stank of dank, root-full richness. Storm lay face down in what seemed to be a peat bog. She groaned and turned over. As she lay there, the squelchy ground beneath her firmed, grew hard and stony. The Tortoise had saved her life yet again. Storm pushed to her feet, wheezing with shock and sore all over, but very much alive.

Something scurried towards her, scuttering over the gravel. Storm drew her knife in a panic, then resheathed it with a sigh as a familiar scolding voice announced Scoundrel. The monkey darted forward and tugged at her trouser leg, muttering and fretting.

"I'm glad you're alive too," Storm said crossly. "But I don't need you to tell me what an idiot I've been. How was I to know the ladder was going to break?"

"Huh! Huh!" It was a contemptuous, sarcastic rebuke. Scoundrel kept tugging until she followed him reluctantly to the bottom of the ladder.

"You want me to go back up there? Are you mad?"

But she had no choice. Other than knocking on the front door and announcing herself, there was no other way to get back into Talon's house. Scoundrel was clever: there must be enough of the ladder left intact. *Maybe only enough to support a monkey!* cautioned her mind-voice. But Storm began the climb again on less than steady legs.

The cling-monkey scampered up before her. As she neared the top, a warning hiss told her to go carefully.

"Like I was going to do anything else," Storm muttered under her breath.

The faint glimmer of starlight showed a gap in the ladder just above her head. Only one rung was broken. She could climb past, with care. But something strange caught her attention... Storm peered closer at the place where the rung had broken away. On one side, the place was splintered, the wood torn as it broke beneath her weight. But on the other she saw a neat stub. This side of the rung hadn't broken. It had been cut.

Someone had sawn this rung in two since she had travelled this way. Someone had tried to kill her, and it could only be one person.

Storm clung to the ladder, closing her eyes as a wave of sickness swept from her head to her feet, turning her legs to mush. Mer hadn't trusted her to keep her word not to help the Pact. Mer had decided that if Storm attempted to return to Talon's house, she would not live to reach her bedroom.

22

Storm woke at least five times in the night from a dream where she was falling: from a cliff, a tree, the mast of the *Wayfarer*. Each time she struggled to keep awake. She needed to think, to plan how she would persuade Talon and the Pact to treat with the rebels. And each time sleep grabbed her by the heels and pulled her back under.

←——————→

Talon's red-and-gold gown rustled as he leaned forward. The leader of the Fifteen Families steepled his fingers and smiled at her over them. His eyes were plump and sticky with greed.

"Time is up, Storm. You must make a commitment to the Pact."

"But I haven't been able to contact all the Elementals!"

"The excuse wears thin. Decision time. Make sure you choose wisely."

Storm had run out of excuses and plans. All that was left was the truth. "I will not help you," she said. "It's wrong."

There was a silken stir from the fifteen councillors who sat at a long table in front of her.

"Come." Talon raised his eyebrows. Still smiling.

He thought she was bargaining! She fought a strange desire to giggle.

"We have established that you are not stupid. You cannot turn your back on the wealth we offer – riches beyond anything you can have dreamed of on your little island! You have seen how the Fifteen live. Don't you want a grand house with servants to wait on your every wish?"

He was so certain. His faith in wealth was unshakeable. She saw that he would think she was lying when she spoke the simple truth, but she said it anyway: "I don't want to live in a home big enough to house a village. My answer is no."

"If it is a question of better terms ... a bigger cut—"

"It is not. You must see that no witch, however powerful, can mend what you have broken. The Fifteen have been robbing their own people for generations!

The people of Bellum were bound to rebel in time. Greed such as yours is not just wrong, it's stupid! If civil war comes to your island, the Pact will lose everything. Worse, Bellum itself may be lost to the enemy! When you have nearly done fighting and killing each other, the Drowned Ones will invade and put those who survive to the sword! I have the word of the great Tortoise itself!"

For a moment, seeing consternation and doubt flash over Talon's face, she thought she had got through to him. But then the councillor's face paled until the painted circles on his cheeks stood out like red chrysanthemums.

The other councillors muttered and shook their heads.

"You are making a very bad mistake," said Talon, and Storm's heart sank. He did not – perhaps *could* not – believe her.

"I am sad to find that you are not as clever as I thought," Talon said. "Perhaps it is merely that you are young and unsophisticated. You haven't had time to understand what you are throwing away. I think we have something to show you that will change your mind."

Talon watched her through narrowed eyes, letting

his words settle. Then he barked at the guard standing beside the door. "Bring him in!"

The guard left the room. A breath later, the door opened and two more guards strode into the room, dragging a bound and bedraggled figure between them. It was Cloud.

His face was bruised, his arms tied behind his back, his tunic dirty and torn. Gripping him by the arm, holding him on his feet, was Tolbar. Her eyes flashed at Storm, as if to say, *This time I win!*

Talon beckoned, and Tolbar shoved Cloud forward, pushing him on to his knees in front of the chief councillor. She stood over the kneeling boy, her hand gripping the hilt of her sword, as the head of the Fifteen rose to his feet and locked eyes with Storm.

"Mistress Storm. You and this boy are accused of unlawful use of magic within the precincts of Bellum Town. The penalties are severe. Do you have anything to say in your defence?"

"Unlawful magic?" He could not mean the attack by the Fire-witch?

"You used Air-magic to vandalise a gaming master's stall. You broke his table and injured two visitors to our island."

So that was it! How long had Talon had this ploy

planned? "My friend and I were attacked by drunkards. I was defending myself and him in the only way I could."

"With magic."

"Magic given to me by the Elementals. Do you persist in picking a quarrel with them? And is it not the responsibility of the town and its councillors to ensure that honest folk may visit your town in peace without being attacked?"

"Vandalism is always illegal. And then there was the damage caused by a certain Fire-witch."

"We did no damage! You say yourself it was the Fire-witch."

"Witnesses report that she was attacking *you*. You obviously have a quarrel with her. That makes you equally responsible for that damage – extensive and expensive damage to the pavement of the square in the resulting earthquake. The Tortoise, I imagine."

"If so," said Storm, "I should consider your own position very carefully before you proceed against me. The Tortoise protects his own. As do the Albatross and Dolphin."

"Perhaps. But this boy is another matter. He is no witch, I think."

"You know he isn't." Storm cast a sideways glance

at Cloud. Someone had beaten him, but he stood stoically, chin raised. As Storm saw the extent of his bruises, anger made her heart thud.

Talon continued: "The charges are serious. His life might be forfeit. But not, of course, if you change your mind and cooperate with the minor tasks we request of you!" He smiled, certain that he had won.

Anger rose, cold as the north wind. Storm turned icy eyes on Talon. "This is how you bargain? With the life of a defenceless boy?"

Her fury burned cold. Chill music circled in her head. The oil lamps flickered. Talon's moustaches began to flap to and fro. The air in the room grew wintry.

She saw the fourteen Pact councillors sitting either side of Talon look at each other in consternation. "I told you it wouldn't work!" Sharp-eyed Waffa, Mer's mother, rose to her feet.

Storm knew that her Air-magic was only waiting for her anger to set it free on a path of destruction. But the other witches had warned her. She remembered what the former Fire-witch had said: "The Salamander grows fat on hate!" She must take care … fight the desire to destroy!

Still the wind whipped around the chamber, which grew colder with each breath Storm took. The Fifteen were shivering, faces contorted with fear. One by one they abandoned their chairs, ran for the door and vanished. All but two. Waffa clung to the table, bracing herself against the wind, her hair whipping around her face, her robes flapping, and berated Talon. "Your entire strategy – concerning not only Yanlin's Weather-witch but your refusal, despite the warnings from several of us, to open negotiations with the rebels – has been a mistake from beginning to end. You are losing your grip, Talon!"

"I don't want to attack you!" Storm spoke with difficulty. Her voice sounded strange: deep and heavy. Frost crystals formed a shining ladder in the air as she spoke, then crackled and fell to the ground with the tinkle of breaking glass. Out of the corner of her eye, Storm noticed Cloud staring at her, eyes huge with terror.

Cloud was afraid of her. Of her, Storm. At the thought, her anger splintered. The icy wind vanished. Storm found she was shaking. Her knees softened and she staggered. When her breath returned to her, she saw a shocked Talon staring at her as though he had never seen her before.

"I … I have misjudged … um … a few details." His voice was choked with disbelief. *Disbelief that he, great*

Talon, could have been wrong, said her mind-voice. "The boy will not be harmed! But he will remain under guard until we negotiate terms."

A freezing wind skirled around the floor; Talon's robes flapped wildly.

"I mistake! The boy need not be imprisoned! And I will consult with my fellow councillors about the rebellion." Talon bowed to Waffa. "We will…" The words issued reluctantly from his lips. "The Pact will begin negotiations with the traitors. And in return…" A flash of the old Talon reappeared.

"In return?" The words came out with a puff of frost.

Talon's face sagged beneath the paint. "In return…" He drew breath, reached deep into his stubbornness. "In return, you must promise not to use your powers against us."

"Cloud goes back to the *Wayfarer*."

"He cannot! Your uncle sailed with the Yanlin fleet the day we took this boy into custody."

So that was why Lake had sailed: fear of further arrests! Storm rubbed her nose. It was surprisingly chilly. She sighed aloud, and this time no frost etched the air from her breath. "Then he stays here, with me."

"Here? In my home?" Talon gazed at Cloud, bruised and barefoot, his coarse sailor's tunic and trousers dirty and torn, and his eyes grew wide with dismay.

"Where else?" asked Storm. "And give him the best guest room in the house!"

23

"This is almost worth getting beat up for!" Cloud was stretched out on a bed even bigger and softer than Storm's. "Hey! Stop that!" He waved a vague hand in the direction of Scoundrel, who was perched on one of the bedposts, tossing peanut hulls at him. "Remind me why you have a cling-monkey?"

"He's not mine. Just visiting." Storm was leaning against the wall, watching Cloud while pretending not to, just in case he was more hurt than he let on. "Did you know the fleet had sailed?"

"No. But I'm not surprised."

"They didn't even try to rescue you."

"Really?" He laughed and sat up, wincing. "Fight the Pact for *me*? I don't think so. Come on, Lake could have lost his entire fleet if the Pact decided to play rough.

You reckon that Pact boss-man is telling the truth when he says he's ready to negotiate with the rebels?"

"I think so. He's scared of losing everything. And of me, I guess." She thought about this. *I don't like being scary*, she told her mind-voice. After a while, she noticed the silence and looked up from her thoughts to see Cloud staring at her, his eyes uncertain.

"That was a pretty amazing trick you did back there. You should have seen yourself…" His voice trailed off. "Or maybe not."

Her smile was bitter; Cloud was scared of her too. "Still want to be an Air-witch?"

"Well … you're a bit more than that, Storm. I don't know what you are, but I wouldn't want to get on the wrong side of you." He attempted a laugh, trying to turn it into a joke. Then his face grew serious. "Why not just finish them off though? If the Pact is the trouble, why not get rid of them? You always back off at the last moment. Anyone else would think you were scared."

She stared at Cloud. This boy wasn't who she had always assumed he was. He wasn't like Thorn. And, she realised, she *was* scared. But not the way he meant.

Storm turned away. "I'm going to my room now. I need some rest." She hadn't slept properly for ages, she realised, and suddenly she was almost too tired to stand on her feet.

"Sure." Cloud's voice was careful.

"Come on, Scoundrel." She left without a backward look. She didn't want Cloud to see how deeply his words had shocked her. The monkey followed her without a sound.

"Fine lot of help you were!" Storm said as she shut her bedroom door behind Scoundrel. "Running off as soon as the guards came to take me to Talon!" She wasn't quite sure what she thought the monkey should have done about it, but it made her feel a tiny bit better to have someone to scold. She tumbled into bed and only had time to wonder if she had imagined seeing the cling-monkey shrug in reply before she was soundly asleep.

←——————→

The old man with the monkey was leaning over her. "Wake up, Storm! Wake up, and I'll let you hold Scoundrel."

Storm struggled to open her eyes. She pushed herself upright at last, and saw that the old man was holding out his cling-monkey. Eagerly she took it in her arms and felt a stab of pure happiness as the tiny creature snuggled beneath her chin.

"His fur is so soft," she said to the old man, unable to express how she was feeling.

"Yes," he said, "but listen to what Scoundrel is telling you.

Quickly now!"

She didn't want anything to disturb the rare happiness filling her. But the old man's voice was urgent.

Reluctantly, Storm bent her head until her ear was near the monkey's face.

The creature reached up, pulled her head closer with its tiny hands and whispered, in the gravelly voice of the Tortoise, "Wake up, Storm! Get out! The Salamander is here!"

←——→

The dream shattered. Storm lurched up in her bed and began to cough. Scoundrel was standing on her pillow, screaming at her. Smoke pressed down, a choking blanket. She heard the hissing crack of greedy flames and looked up to see an inferno. Sparks showered from the ceiling. The house was on fire!

Storm froze for several heartbeats, then her body sprang into action almost without her willing it. She rolled off the bed, keeping low to the ground, away from the choking smoke.

"Get out, Scoundrel! Run!" She saw the monkey race to the open window and leap towards the nearest tree. He was safe. She crawled to the table, grabbed her possessions and made her way towards the door. The air was still breathable near the floor. The Salamander hadn't won yet!

She had nearly reached the door when something groaned overhead, and, with an explosion of sparks, part of the ceiling crashed down into the room behind her. Storm looked over her shoulder and saw that the bed had disappeared in a column of fire.

She shot out of the room, scrabbled to her feet, ran to Cloud's door, and flung it open. "Fire! Fire! Cloud, wake up!" The fire seemed to be centred over her bedroom, but flames were even now leaping across the ceiling of the corridor, spreading with every moment. Could the fire be tracking her like a hound?

The lump in the bed groaned. Raised a reluctant head.

"The house is on fire! Get out!"

Cloud shouted in alarm and jumped out of bed. Seeing he was properly awake, Storm turned and ran from the room in case the fire really was chasing her. She must get out of the building at once.

She had no idea how many people were asleep in the house. Storm shrieked "Fire!" as she ran, banging on each door she passed. She whirled out of the main entrance just as a guard came running. "Fire!" she cried unnecessarily. In the distance, an alarm bell began to ring.

"Get away," the guard ordered. "Away from the

house. All of you!"

Guests and servants were straggling out now, looking bewildered and terrified. She saw Talon leading a tearful Betaan by the hand.

A dozen other guards and officials had come running and were busy forming a human chain, dipping buckets in the nearest pond.

"Everyone is out," an official told Talon. "The fire is only in the guest wing. But it's caught hold. I don't think we can put it out."

The moonlight dimmed. Storm looked up to see the shadow of a giant bird cross in front of the moon. She was a fool! She tried to collect her wits, to calm herself enough to find the music of Air and Water. Here she was – a Weather-witch – letting the house burn to the ground!

She edged away from the weeping, complaining people who had poured out of the house and put her belongings on a garden seat. It would be best if she could make this appear a natural thunderstorm.

The Albatross was waiting. As soon as she listened properly, Air-music filled her mind and ran through her blood. She thought about the wooden flute, but she had never tried to use one. Then it was too late: she was inside the music and it was inside her.

Storm felt the air thicken, grow restless. She felt the electricity gather high overhead. She felt water being sucked out of the sea in sheets to thicken the clouds. The night sky congealed, grew black as mud. *Now!* thought Storm.

The heavens opened and a deluge descended upon the burning house, the guards and officials, on Talon, Cloud and Betaan, on the raging fire.

24

Rain beat down. Fire hissed and spat. Water soaked the wooden roof and drove the flames back until they dwindled and disappeared, leaving only the stink of half-burnt wood and wet ash.

Almost at once, the clouds thinned, the stars and moon shone down in a puddle of light. Storm wished she had tried the flute; there had been nothing subtle about that magic!

"Thank the Ancestors!" exclaimed Betaan. She was shivering. Everyone was drenched to the skin.

"I think it is the Weather-witch we should thank," said Talon. "Is that not right, Mistress Storm?"

"I did what I could," she said, with a polite bow. Talon studied her with a calculating look. *He won't stop trying to control you. He'll wriggle out of negotiating with the rebels at the first opportunity*, her mind-voice warned.

The stares and awed exclamations of the other guests and servants began to make her feel awkward. Storm gathered her things and began to walk away into the garden.

"Do not wander far, Weather-witch!" Talon had noticed. "The damage is limited to one wing. We will have another room prepared for you before long."

Storm gave a quick bow as answer and hurried away.

"Storm! Wait up!" It was Cloud.

Ancestors! She pretended not to hear and hurried away. She wanted to be alone to think. The Salamander had struck out at her even here – where the Earth-witch had thought she would be safe. If Scoundrel hadn't woken her... Storm shivered. Nowhere on Bellum was safe.

Cloud caught up with her. "Hey! Didn't you hear me?" He was soaked through, his nightclothes dripping and his hair plastered to his head. And he was buzzing with excitement. "That was an amazing bit of magic! What's up, Storm? Are you all right? You're shivering." His eyes narrowed with disbelief. "Are you *scared*?"

Unconscious scorn laced his words. Storm saw his thoughts as though he had spoken them aloud: *Why did the Elementals give her the magic? She's weak and cowardly. I should have been the Weather-witch!*

"Are you all right?" he asked again.

"I'm fine. Have you seen Scoundrel?"

"The monkey?" Cloud wrinkled his nose in amazement. "Talon's house nearly burns down and you're worried about a dumb cling-monkey?"

She clenched her jaw. Shouting wouldn't help. "Could you keep these for me?" She held out her journal and the parcel. "I bought a toy boat as a grave present for Thorn, and I don't want it to get broken. Can you keep it safe, please?"

"Storm, come on…" His expression told her that looking after a toy boat didn't seem terribly heroic.

"Just for a little while. I won't be long."

Cloud sighed. "Can I have a look at the boat?"

She smiled, relieved. "Absolutely. It's amazing so take care of it, please."

Storm left him unwrapping the parcel and hurried into the garden until she was out of sight. The fire had not been a coincidence. Not after that dream! Once more the Earth spirit had saved her. And where *was* Scoundrel? Worry wrinkled her brow, and Storm called for the cling-monkey as she walked. No scampering shape came running to her out of the moon-shadows. *He made it out of the window*, said her mind-voice. *Scoundrel can look after himself.*

Storm walked deep into the garden, as far away from the smoking house and the stink of damp soot and charcoal as she could get. At last she stopped beside a small lake. Moonlight fell out of the sky into the water, and she saw a large carp circling peacefully, its body gleaming white in the moon's beam. As she watched, entranced, the fish jigged sideways and its body spasmed. It stiffened and floated to the surface.

Shocked, Storm fell to her knees to see if the beautiful fish was really dead. Something blazed overhead, searing the air where her head had been a breath ago. There was a blinding flash, the smell of burning, and a small tree on the far side of the lake burst into flame.

The carp, suddenly very much alive, flipped over and dived towards the depths. Instinctively, Storm filled her lungs and plunged headlong into the water after it. She heard fire crack on the bank where she had been kneeling only a heartbeat before and kicked even harder towards the safety of deep water. Once she was well below the surface, she somersaulted until she was head skywards and peered up towards the world of air, trying to locate her attacker. She was aware of the white-gold carp swimming slowly round and round her.

Thank you, Dolphin! Storm spared a moment to express gratitude to the Elemental, even though her heart was trying to beat a path out of her chest.

As for her attacker, Storm had no doubt who was waiting up in the air to strike again the moment she surfaced. If she was going to survive she must do Water-magic more difficult and complex than any she had ever managed. *Help me again, Dolphin, or I die*, Storm pleaded.

Still the carp circled round and round. Was that a sign? Storm's lungs began to hurt. In a few more heartbeats she would be forced to surface. Far above, she thought she saw something move in the moonlit air: a reddish glimmer.

Storm tried to clear her mind and let the music of water flow into her. Slowly at first, then more easily, Water-music filtered into her mind until she felt shining-full of its mysterious beauty. She had an image of herself, glowing white-gold like the carp.

Storm submerged herself in the bitter-sweet beauty of Water's slippery, tricksy nature. Almost, she felt she could grasp some meaning ... understand a fragment of its elemental pattern. She took hold of the single thread of the pattern she had seen, and began carefully to weave a small waterspout around her. The water at the bottom of the pond began to rotate. The hardest part was keeping the surface of the little lake still. She must trick her enemy into thinking she was dead. That Fire had won…

Now! Storm let the water take her. She rose inside the eye of the spout as it exploded to the surface, draining the lake. Storm stood motionless in the centre of the waterspout as it whirled around her. Her head was level with the tallest tree branches. She peered through the streaming wall of water full of weeds, small stones and hapless fish, looking for her enemy.

A red-clothed figure writhed on the ground a dozen paces from shore. The woman pushed to her feet, shrieking curses. She was drenched with water, plastered with mud, her silk tunic ruined, her plaits dripping. The witch raised clenched fists towards the waterspout. A bolt of flame shot from the woman's hands. Storm smelt heat and burning, felt the fire bolt strike the spout.

The water wall around her shuddered and Storm lurched downwards, arms and legs clawing at nothing. Steam rose into the air along with a fierce hissing, as though of a giant serpent. Storm found enough breath to scream once, then the water caught hold once more and buoyed her up. Quickly, before the enemy could strike again, she lashed out with a whip of icy water. It hit the Fire-witch with a sound like a lightning strike, and the woman flew through the air and crashed into some bushes.

The enemy was now too far away to be fought with water. Storm released the waterspout, leaping on to the ground as it sank back into the lake, and readied her Air-magic.

She ran towards the figure she could see pushing itself upright. As she ran, Storm sent a wind swirling low and fierce. The wind caught the Fire-witch just as the woman turned and raised her fists again. Storm felt a moment's respect for her enemy's toughness, and considerable fear. If her Air-magic failed her, she would die.

The wind hit the witch, and the woman was lifted off her feet. Storm watched, appalled at the power she had unleashed, as a small tornado sucked the woman up into the sky – into its whirling heart – and tore through the garden, digging a deep channel into the ground as it went.

"Stop!" shrieked Storm. "Don't kill her!" But the whirlwind swept on. This magic was none of hers; the Elementals had taken over. The tornado burst through the garden wall with an explosion of stone that showered fragments of rock and dirt high into the air. On it went, until it disappeared in the direction of the sea.

Storm stood staring after, left alone with the trail of devastation. Something made her glance upwards, and she saw the Albatross flying overhead, its wingspan nearly as wide as the sky.

Later, Storm couldn't remember how she got back to the pond, or how long she had stood there, staring down at the carp slowly circling in the moonlight. At last, she heard the sound of people running towards her. Heard gasps of shock; commands and arguments. Finally, someone approached slowly.

"You will come with us, please, Weather-witch. The chief councillor wishes to speak to you most urgently. Make no sudden moves, if you please."

Wearily, Storm turned to face the speaker. It was a silver-haired official. The woman's face was creased with shock. Two archers stood either side of her, arrows notched and bows drawn. Storm sighed. She had lost this roll of the dice. It was clear that Talon now knew the secret she had been trying to keep from him – that the Salamander was trying to kill her.

25

"So this attack, which has destroyed half my house and devastated an ancient garden planted by our honoured ancestors, has nothing to do with you? Is that what you expect me to believe?"

Talon was not looking as elegant as usual. He still wore his damp, sooty nightclothes beneath a robe tugged on and belted haphazardly. His forehead needed shaving and his hair was straggling down his back. Every word and gesture spoke of outrage that he should be pulled so rudely from his bed. That seemed to offend him almost as much as the fact that his ancestral house was damaged. "Well? Do you still claim not to know the witch who attacked you?"

"I didn't see them closely," Storm lied again.

"You don't deny that the fire started in the wing

where you were sleeping."

"Of course not. But I wasn't the only guest there."

"Or that you put out the fire?"

"Given your hospitality, Councillor, how could I do less?" Storm made him a small, formal bow to take away the sting of irony in her words. She was so tired! When would this endless questioning finish?

Talon ran his hands through his hair and asked, for the hundredth time, "Why did you go into the garden?"

"I was looking for my monkey. When I reached the pond, I spotted someone on a nearby path. It was clear by the way they moved that they wanted to keep their presence hidden. Until that moment, I had thought the guest-house fire had been an accident." Lying had become uncomfortably easy. "Foolishly, I called out for the intruder to stop. And ... they attacked me with fire."

"So you say." Talon rubbed a weary hand over his head, tangling his hair even more. "Indeed, so you say."

"Does any other explanation make sense?"

Talon frowned. "Except that this is not the first time the woman has tried to kill you. Come, Storm. You must grant that I'm no fool. Who is this enemy of yours? Be warned: she may have survived. We have searched the harbour, even dragged it with nets, but we have not found a body."

Storm shuddered. She didn't know if she was relieved or terrified by the news that the Fire-witch might still be alive.

Talon smiled triumphantly. "As I thought. You have somehow made a mortal enemy of the Salamander! Or, at least, one of his most powerful servants. So … what does that fact mean to me? To the Pact?"

He drummed his fingernails on the table, and Storm saw a greedy look enter his eyes. "Your arguments with the Elementals are your own affair. I think it best if the Pact stays well out of that. But damage has been done, and that *is* your responsibility. You brought your magical warfare into my house, and now you must repay me for the devastation it wrought – both to my house and to the Pact's historical and priceless garden! That is only fair."

"But…" Storm stared, appalled.

"If you had not carelessly wandered off, if you had not engaged in a magic fight with the Fire-witch, the garden would still be intact. As it is…" He waved his hands and shook his head with mock sorrow. "Conservatively, I estimate that repairing the damage would cost all the goods the Yanlin fleet could send for at least, oh, ten years. Which would, of course be a disaster for your island."

"Ten years!"

"Dozens of rare and irreplaceable trees – some hundreds of years old – have been ripped from the earth. At least one ancient bridge has been destroyed. It will take a generation before the garden is restored to its former glory, if it ever is! We may even have to send an expedition to the Outer Sea in search of replacement seedlings."

Despite his dramatic words, Talon did not seem upset. Indeed, the councillor's moustaches spread in a merry smile. "I think we have no choice but to keep you working for us for a period of three years, as an indentured servant. Oh, do not worry: your duties will not involve policing rebels. I and my colleagues have taken your words to heart. We shall open negotiations with the trait— With those who petition the Pact in an appropriate manner.

"You, however, will work without pay, guarding the fleets that come to trade on Bellum and protecting us all from the Drowned Ones.

"We will give you comfortable lodgings – not, ahem, in my house – and servants, as befits your status. If, after three years working for the Pact, you wish to continue as our partner, well … that would be most acceptable." Talon smoothed his wayward hair back from his forehead and his eyebrows rose in hoops of happiness.

She could freeze him into an ice statue where he sat. But only if the Albatross wanted her to, which she doubted. Talon's death would not solve the problem of Bellum Island.

She tried to salvage something: "Cloud is free to leave? And my uncle free to return with the fleet to Bellum? To finish trading? You will not punish Yanlin with even more taxes because of my ... misfortune?"

"But of course!" Talon smiled broadly, waggled his crimson-nailed hands to show his disinterest. Having acquired his Weather-witch, he could afford small gestures of magnanimity.

←——————→

Two days later, at dawn, the messenger boat sailed into Bellum harbour, followed by the *Wayfarer*. Storm met with her uncle and his second master in her new quarters, in the official Pact guest house. Which, she noted, was on the opposite side of the square from Talon's house.

"I think he arranged the attack himself!" Lake raged, pacing round and round her somewhat smaller, plainer room. "I wouldn't put it past these pampered civil servants! The man wouldn't know a bowsprit from a yardarm! Never did an honest day's work in his life!"

"Well, well." Foam squatted with his back against the wall, watching his captain pace back and forth, as Lake had been doing ever since they had arrived. "What can't be helped must be endured." The second master cast an agonised look at Storm, who sat nearby, waiting for her uncle's anger to wear itself out. She wished he would hurry up about it. Each word was an arrow in her heart. Her people must leave her behind.

The *Wayfarer* had finished trading. It would now begin the homeward journey. She would be left alone in this strange place full of danger. And there was no help for it: none at all.

"It's only three years, Uncle," Storm said, when Lake paused to draw breath. "It will pass quickly enough." The three years stretched out before her like a lifetime. She wouldn't see Minnow, or Auntie Briathe, or Teanu. She wouldn't be able to set foot on Yanlin. Or visit her mother's grave. And at the thought of Dain, Storm's resolve broke, and she hid her face in her hands.

Someone shuffled near and a hand patted her awkwardly on the shoulders. "There, there, Storm. Don't cry, child. Please." Uncle Lake sounded so miserable that Storm found the strength to stifle her tears. She took a deep gulping breath.

"I am sorry, Uncle. I do not mean to distress you."

"I'm not going." Cloud, who had been standing silently all this time, spoke at last.

"What do you mean, boy?" Lake frowned at his apprentice. "Of course you're sailing with the fleet."

"I'm going to stay here with Storm."

"You're my apprentice. Your time is mine! Besides, what use would you be?" Lake's words were scathing. "You've no magic. No skills at all, except eating and sleeping and getting into trouble!"

"Perhaps." Cloud's face was red with embarrassment. "But I can be company, if nothing else. Someone from home. A friend."

"And who's going to feed you?" asked Foam. "Don't expect the Pact to pay for your keep, for they won't."

"And nor will I!" growled Lake.

"I'll work for my food!" Cloud said. "I can carry and tote as well as anyone else."

"Well…" Uncle Lake turned to Storm. "I'm properly confounded. It's up to you, Storm. Do you want the boy? If he'll be a bother, I'll take him with me, willing or no! Just say what you want."

What she wanted. The idea made her feel like

laughing … or crying. Everything she'd ever treasured or yearned for, everything she had ever needed – her father, her mother, Thorn, to be normal – she had lost all of them, one by one.

She gazed at Cloud, feeling as confounded as her uncle. This was the act of a true friend. He must have forgiven her for being, in his eyes, weak and cowardly. Part of her rejoiced. She *was* weak. The frightened part of her wanted his company, to keep away loneliness and fear of what the future held. But too many of her friends and loved ones had died already.

It was on the tip of her tongue to tell Lake to take Cloud with him when she saw unshed tears shining in her shipmate's eyes. And suddenly she was imagining herself as Cloud – a boy desperate to do this one thing: this simple, ordinary thing that would make him, for a brief time, extraordinary – more than just a cabin boy from a tiny island few had ever heard of.

"I…" Storm hesitated, waiting for her mother's spirit to guide her. The message came at once. She could almost hear Dain's voice telling her that such gifts – given from the heart, gifts of self-sacrifice – must always be accepted, even if the cost was high.

"Yes, please. I would like Cloud to stay."

26

When Talon was informed that Cloud would be Storm's companion, he waved both hands in dismissal. "Nothing to do with the Pact."

In the end, Storm was able to persuade him to let Cloud work as a guest-house servant in return for food and lodging. He would sleep in the attics with the other servants. An official marched him off to his new lodgings.

Storm watched them go with relief then retreated to her room. Days after the Fire-witch's attack, her body still felt as if someone had beaten her with a rope. She was sore from an excess of magic and heartache. She lay down on another too-big, too-soft bed and knew no more until a knock on her door announced the arrival of her lunch.

Storm pushed away the light quilt; she was hot and dizzy with sleep. "Come in!"

The door swung wide, too wide. It bashed into the wall and rebounded on the figure entering the room. "Blast it!" Cloud grabbed the covered plate which was sliding off the tray he carried. He closed the door behind him with more care and turned to face Storm, looking as awkward as she felt. "Um. Your lunch, St— Mistress."

"Don't call me that! And put that down before you drop it."

"Sorry." Cloud scurried to set the tray on the low table below the window. It clattered down, the bowl slopping a brownish liquid. Storm sighed.

"You will never make a servant."

"I'm rubbish, aren't I?"

"Yes. And if you call me 'Mistress' again I'll…"

Cloud grinned.

"Have you had lunch?" Storm asked.

"Not yet. We servants eat after you guest folk."

"Well, have that. I'm not hungry."

"I don't believe it. You must have used up masses of energy fighting off that Fire-witch. Eat!"

Once she had taken the first spoonful of soup, Storm found she was, after all, very hungry, and soon scraped the bowl clean. She put the spoon down reluctantly and frowned at Cloud. "Are you sure about all this? The fleet sails tomorrow for home. You can still change your mind."

Cloud shook his head. "You may be the witch — although I still don't know why the Elementals chose you over me…" He smiled broadly, as if it was a joke. "But you can't keep all the fun to yourself!"

Storm shrugged, keeping things casual. She and Cloud would never agree about what it meant to be brave, and his jealousy of her magic seemed worse than ever. Had she made a mistake, agreeing to let him stay? "Have you seen Scoundrel?"

"The monkey hasn't come back?"

"I haven't seen him since the fire."

"Um. Do you think…"

"No!" She was surprised at how upset she felt at the suggestion. "He's alive. I saw him climb out of the window."

"Sure." Cloud bent his head, busily tidying up. "Someone else has disappeared."

"Who?"

"That girl you hung out with. Mer. Some are saying she was in league with the Fire-witch. Anyway, they're looking for her, but no luck yet. You need to stay indoors for a while, until they catch the witch. No going off into town by yourself, understood?"

"Since when are you the boss of me, Cloud?" Shock at the thought that Mer might be working, not with the Drowned Ones, but with the Fire-witch, made her snap before she could stop herself. But Cloud almost seemed to welcome her anger, nodding with approval.

"I'm serious! You may be the witch, but I know what I'm talking about."

He was so happy in his self-appointed role of protector of magic that she softened. "I promise, all right? Now get back to work before they beat you. I want to sleep some more."

But she tossed and turned as sleep refused to come. Could it be true? Had Mer been working with the Fire-witch? Or had she finally decided to join the rebels in body as well as spirit? Maybe it was simply that Mer knew Storm had found the sawn rung and was frightened to meet her.

When at last exhaustion tipped her into sleep, Storm slept badly, half expecting another attempt on her life by the Salamander. What had happened to the Fire-witch? The woman could be dead, her body washed up on a distant beach. It depended on how far the whirlwind had carried her, and that depended on the whim of the Albatross.

She woke before dawn, dressed, strapped her knife around her waist and hung the flute the Air-witch had given her around her neck. She had made a soft leather case for it, which hung by a hemp cord.

She would visit the small lake to watch the white carp swim. She didn't want to be noticed by the guest-house officials and guards, so Storm opened her window and swung herself down on to the ground. In a few heartbeats she was strolling through the garden.

She stood beside the lake for a long time, watching the white carp circle beneath the water, wondering if the Dolphin would give her a sign. Or the Albatross. Was the danger over? Was the witch dead?

But none of the Elementals spoke. The carp was plainly an ordinary fish, and had nothing to tell her either. Only the line dug through the earth like the mark of an enormous hoe – and the corpses of blasted and uprooted trees and shrubs tossed either side of it – testified that the night of fire had really happened.

If the Elementals weren't going to help her, she would have to help herself. Storm looked for a spot to practise the flute the Air-witch had given her. An enormous yew tree stood beside the lake. Its lower branches bent low and swept the ground, forming a green tent.

Storm pushed through into a hidden chamber circling the tree's trunk. She settled cross-legged on the thick brown carpet of shed needles and drew the flute from its case. She was eager to try tiny, precise magic. Remembering the Air-witch's trick with the paper whirligigs, she put the flute to her lips and began to blow.

Soon Storm found that it was only in those moments when she could stop worrying – about the Fire-witch, about Scoundrel, about Talon – that her Air-magic was completely under control. After many failed attempts, she managed a new level of concentration and suddenly the needles rose from the ground one by one as though strung like beads upon an invisible string. They played follow-my-leader, circling in a slow fairy dance around her head, up to the ceiling of thick brown-red branches and back down. Storm watched them in delight and the flute warbled sweetly. Gentle magic! She had done it at last!

Then a movement somewhere above her in the tree made her think of Scoundrel. A blast of wind sent the tree's branches flapping, and the dancing needles flew away in all directions.

"Ancestors!" Storm muttered and looked up, trying to quell hope but not quite succeeding. It must have been a bird; there was no sign of the cling-monkey. She sighed, brushed needles from her hair and put away the flute.

She ought to practise some more, but suddenly her heart wasn't in it.

You may need all your magic soon, warned her mind-voice. *The Salamander has not finished with you.*

Storm frowned, rubbed her nose. Later. She would go and sit beside the pond again, and watch the white carp circle. The loss of Dain was sharp today.

Storm crawled out from beneath the sweeping branches of the yew, stood straight and stretched, unbending her spine. Head back she saw, lodged high in the branches of the tree above her, the shaft of an arrow.

Her heart lurched. She dropped to the ground, wormed back beneath the tree. Heart pounding, she crouched, waiting for an unknown enemy to attack again. Many breaths she waited, fear dry in her throat. Nothing happened. The garden birds sang. Squirrels chased each other across the sun-patches between the trees. At last, Storm made herself accept the fact that there would not be another arrow-shot.

Had this one, in fact, been aimed at her? It would have taken incredible luck for it to penetrate the thick needle-clad branches of the tree with enough force to hurt. And it had been shot high in the tree in any case. Nowhere near where she had been hiding. Storm jumped to her feet and began to climb. The thick branches were closely spaced, the needles sharp. It was an awkward, prickly, breathless climb. But she reached the arrow, pulled it free and, one-handed, half climbed, half fell back to earth.

Storm stood in the dappled green light beneath the yew and unrolled the parchment wrapped around the arrow shaft. She gasped aloud when she saw it was a piece torn from her own journal! How? And then she saw that the torn fragment was part of the page that recorded her journey over the rooftops with Mer.

Storm turned the fragment over and saw, drawn in charcoal lines on the reverse, a diagram of the centre of the city. It was a crude copy of the map Betaan had shown her. The tavern where she had met her uncle and Foam the day she escaped from Tolbar was circled. And beside it someone had drawn the mark that meant high moon, the middle of the night – a crescent moon perched on the point of a vertical arrow.

Storm frowned as she considered what to do. This message was meant for her and it wasn't difficult to interpret. Someone wanted her to meet them at the tavern at high moon. Tonight? It must be. And as to the person … it must be Mer herself. The other girl must have seen it often in her old room. Storm chewed her bottom lip as she thought.

Dangerous to go. But impossible not to. Mer was her route to the rebels. She needed to convince them that the Fifteen recognised the need for reform. Talon might be reluctant, but he was leader in name only now. She wondered how Mer would feel about the fact that it was her mother, Waffa, who had taken control.

And what if it's a trap? asked her mind-voice. *What if you're wrong and she does work with the Fire-witch? What if she's been paid to betray you?*

Then I will find out. And what will be will be. No more waiting! I can't keep hidden here in the Pact quarter, hoping my enemies won't hurt me.

Decision made, Storm stabbed the arrow into the deep litter of decaying yew needles and reached for her flute. Time to practise. More than just her life depended upon her magic. Dain had taught her to always keep trying, no matter how difficult things got or how many mistakes she made. *I won't give up, Ma! I promise.*

27

The star rose into the night sky, green as a the eye of a strangle snake. She had been ready for a countless time, crouched beside her open window, watching the Snake Star emerge from the sea.

Nearly time. Storm rubbed her nose. So much could go wrong. She shook her head. She had decided: she would meet with Mer. She strapped on her knife, slung the flute around her neck.

Storm pushed open the casement, slipped over the sill and dropped lightly to the ground. It was safer to leave by the window: less risk of waking another guest. And, although she didn't think there were guest-house officials about, she could be wrong. Keeping low, she darted from shadow to shadow, keeping trees and shrubs between her and the gatehouse.

Too dangerous to try to sneak into Talon's garden to use the route out of the garden Mer had shown her. But there was another way she could escape. The whirlwind that had carried off the Fire-witch had destroyed part of the wall around the central garden. She had scouted it out after lunch, while pretending to stroll around the garden. A rough wooden fence had been erected until repairs were made, but for someone used to scaling sea cliffs to collect gulls' eggs, it would be an easy climb. As long as the guards posted in the guardhouse didn't spot her.

Storm crouched in the shadow beneath an old spreading tree for a long time, watching the stretch of the broken wall and listening to her heart pounding in her ears. No sign of a watcher. She took a deep breath, gathered herself and sprinted forward, feeling as though the rising moon was aiming its light directly at her. She leapt for the first plank, pulled herself up and was at the top and over before she could breathe twice.

She was in an alley so narrow it was nearly a gutter. The land to her left fell away towards the sea, and in the moonlight she could clearly see the opening cut through the scrubby hillside, which ended a few paces away in a sheer cliff. Storm walked to the edge; peered down. Far below was a rocky spit, and then the sea. She heard the waves pounding the shingle spit. Surely no one could have survived that fall ... unless the tornado had carried the Fire-witch all the way to the water before releasing its victim. Storm shivered, and began the journey to the Merry Whale.

It was fast approaching high moon. The Snake Star was nearly overhead. On Yanlin, the town would be deserted, the townsfolk asleep in their houses, but the streets near the main square were half full of loiterers and drunks going in and out of the many taverns lining the streets, signed by the yellow glow of lanterns hung above their doors.

At least she need not worry about being noticed. Sailors of all ages swarmed the streets. Even so, she ducked into doorways three times to watch in case she was being followed. Nothing. Ignoring her feelings of unease, Storm strode as quickly as she could the rest of the way to the tavern.

The inside of the Merry Whale was gloomy. Tallow lamps oozed yellow smoke and filled the room with distorting shadows. Storm stood against a wall near the entrance until her eyes adjusted. She spotted Mer almost at once, even though her face was bare of paint and her clothes were made of hemp instead of silk. The girl sat at a small table by herself. Her face flashed relief as their eyes met.

Storm walked as normally as she could across the room. Her heart was thudding, but now that she was here, she found she was strangely calm. *What will be will be*, agreed her mind-voice.

"Didn't really expect to see you." Mer gestured to the mat beside her and, with a last careful look around the room, Storm sat down.

"Why are we here? And why did you leave home?"

"For the same reason." Mer leaned nearer, lowered her voice. "I've decided it was a good thing I didn't kill you on the stairs. Sorry about that, by the way. In fact, I think the Ancestors may have sent you to Bellum to help us."

Storm felt her mouth open. Was it really going to be so easy? "Are there many of you? Are you organised?"

"As many as aren't too deep in drink or poverty to care. Or who aren't in the pay of the Pact. Of course, we have to keep ourselves secret. If the Pact scents the slightest dissent it strikes with the viciousness of a spit-snake. Many have disappeared. Even though we are powerless to do more than watch and talk and … hate. We need a champion. Someone with the power to fight the Pact. We need you!"

"It may not come to fighting. I have news…"

Something was wrong. Mer's face had gone pale as parchment. She was staring at something behind them. Fear had flickered to life in her eyes. "The innkeeper! She keeps looking at us and pretending not to. There's a reward out for me. I think I've been spotted."

Carefully, Storm turned her head toward the spot the other girl was watching. And saw the tavern keeper, a tall strong woman with muscular arms, staring intently at the door. The woman's eyes swivelled to them, flinched from Storm's gaze and flicked back to the door.

"We need to get out of here," Storm said.

But just then she saw a look of relief flash across the tavern keeper's face. Storm's stomach lurched. Too late!

Two Pact guards pushed through the door and the tavern keeper pointed at Mer. The guards had their batons out. No swords or knives. And only two, a man and a woman. The tavern keeper hadn't known who she was informing on, and that meant they had a chance.

Storm readied her magic as she pulled the flute from its pouch, hoping her practice earlier in the day had paid off.

"Stay close!" she told Mer as she grabbed a mindful

of music out of the air and used it to fashion a slender battering ram of wind. "Just the doorway, please," she muttered, and blew into the flute. The air in the room vibrated. Storm took a deep breath and shrilled a fierce note that grabbed the column of air and rammed it at the man and woman stalking towards them.

The air struck the guards with a heavy thudding noise and sent them flying. Storm grabbed Mer's arm and pushed her towards the door. Too late, she saw another pair of guards waiting outside. One of them grabbed at Mer, but the tall girl kicked out and knocked her attacker off his feet. Storm fluted a blast of notes that sent the guards tumbling along the ground, shouting and hollering.

Just the guards, she noted. None of the bystanders or drunks. Even the inn sign overhead barely swayed in its brackets. Nice and precise. Storm turned to Mer with a satisfied grin. "Are you all right?"

Mer started to nod. Then she gazed over Storm's shoulder, and her face froze. *More guards!* thought Storm. But she was wrong.

"Run!" shouted Mer. "The witch!" She gave Storm an almighty push that sent her spinning across the road. The flute flew out of her hand into the darkness.

Storm felt a searing flash of heat behind her. Something scorched her hair. The Fire-witch had found her again!

28

Storm was already moving, racing away on legs made fast by fear. Dodging, weaving, readying the fiercest magic she could rip from the air around her. She wouldn't let the Fire-witch kill her, not without a fight!

She glimpsed a thin, red-robed figure standing in the middle of the square. Mer had vanished. At least now she knew the other girl had not been working with the Salamander's child. The Fire-witch might have been trailing Mer for days, or even followed the guards here. The most likely explanation is that she had been keeping watch on Talon's guest house and followed Storm herself to the tavern. It didn't matter. Staying alive did! Another fireball screamed towards her, but Storm was already somewhere else.

As she ran, she drew more and more air to her. The

light above the tavern began to sway wildly, illuminating a chaos of terror as drinkers and passers-by ran for their lives. The night was full of screams and wails. One of the guards that had come to arrest Mer ran past, shouting, sword raised. She heard his death cry as fire licked forward, hungry. The other guard retreated, frantically notching an arrow to her bow.

The witch will only burn the shafts in mid-air. Storm reached the edge of the square. By some instinct, she swerved suddenly, and the house that had been in front of her only a breath before burst into flames.

No space. No time. *Albatross! Aid me.* The Dolphin could not help. The Tortoise would help if it felt it necessary, no doubt. And the fact that the ground did not shift beneath her feet gave Storm courage. The Earth spirit wasn't intervening, which meant it had faith in her magic. She could defeat the Salamander's agent if she was brave enough. If she believed…

A guard had just died because of her. Storm turned to face the Fire-witch.

The woman was standing at the centre of the square. Fire danced in her long hair, flowed down her arms to drip like molten lava on to the pavement at her feet. Fire raged inside the witch's body – she stood like a human sun illuminating the night.

The Fire-witch laughed as she saw Storm turn. She raised both her clenched fists, pointed them at her prey.

"This will stop!" Storm roared, and her open mouth released the wind-blast of her anger and fear, channelling it as well as she could without the flute. Wind poured out of her mouth, fierce as a typhoon, cold as frost. Unforgiving as the ever-ice on the high mountains, Storm's battering ram of wind flew at the Fire-witch.

It met the fireball head on. For less than the time than it takes for a cling-monkey's heart to beat once, the two forces struggled, neither making way. Still Storm screamed her anger. Her teeth ached from cold. She lost feeling in her hands and feet, then her legs. Ice formed on her body, crawled up her arms and legs, froze her hair. She saw it creep down her forehead towards her eyes until it glazed them over and the Fire-witch was only an orange glow on the other side of a cocoon of ice. The pain of the cold was so intense her scream was now one of agony.

And then, with a loud, vibrating boom that shattered the ice covering Storm's eyes, the wind she had magicked swallowed the fireball and rushed on towards the witch. Storm watched the woman cry out, cower on the ground. She saw a dome of fire cover the crouching figure like a shield. Then the fire-dome and the witch were engulfed by the wind and swept away.

Storm stopped screaming. She was empty of air, empty of magic. She lacked even the strength necessary to close her mouth. Her eyes, which seemed the only part of her able to move, searched the darkness for any sign of the Fire-witch.

The only thing left of the witch was the devastation Storm had wrought fighting her: lanterns, signs and doors torn from buildings, carts overturned. Even the small crumbling fountain skulking in a corner of the square had been plucked from the ground and lay broken on its side, water spraying from a broken pipe. It formed a stream which meandered, black and wet, through the rubble, like a trickle of blood.

Storm felt her legs unfreeze. Pain redoubled as her blood warmed and feeling came back into her legs and arms. When the blood reached her fingers, she screamed. She felt herself sway, fall as a grey blankness swam up over her eyes and blotted out everything.

←——————→

Something soft and warm and smelling of monkey was stroking her face.

"Scoundrel?" Hope pushed back the grey blanket pressing on her. Storm opened her eyes. It was night-time, and she was lying on her side on damp pavement.

Memory returned and, with a gasp, Storm sat up. Scoundrel was crouched on his haunches beside her, peering into her face. The monkey seemed reassured by what he saw. He immediately grabbed Storm's hand and began to tug, squealing at her to get up.

Storm gazed into the dark. People were scurrying around, carrying torches, shouting. All seemed confusion, but there was no sign of the Fire-witch. Storm realised she couldn't have been unconscious for more than a few moments. And that Scoundrel was right: it was time to get out of here!

At least one person was dead because of her. The square was a scene of devastation: buildings damaged by wind, half burned by fire. There were bound to be more injuries, perhaps deaths. The town guards would be here soon, and if she was found she would be in danger of permanent incarceration by the Pact. She could hardly blame Talon, looking about her. She felt sick with guilt.

Storm pushed to her feet, fought off a spell of dizziness. Where she had been lying was a puddle of melting ice water. Shivering, she stumbled after Scoundrel, content to let the monkey lead her where it would. "I'm in your hands, Tortoise," she whispered as she turned her back on the latest proof that the Salamander seriously wanted her dead.

She had to go slowly. Her legs did not seem to work as they used to, refusing to follow one another in a straight line. Storm staggered side to side, rebounding off walls in the dark alleyways, pausing to rest against the hard brick of sleeping houses.

Her heart was stuttering, skipping beats. She felt ill to her core. Storm hadn't felt this unwell since catching the wasting fever, when she was still a child. She had nearly died. Dain had nursed her to health. So long ago. Perhaps she would see Ma soon, in the land of the spirits. Part of her wanted to stop right here, leaning against a stranger's house. To lie down and not get up again.

Scoundrel grabbed her trouser leg, tugged, chattering angrily. His claws scratched and the pain roused her. Storm sighed, took a deep breath to combat the pain and nausea she knew were waiting, and pushed away from the wall. She began to walk, following the Earth-witch's monkey into the night.

The night darkened further, and Storm looked up to see the moon had fallen at last into the sea. Dawn was still far off but the night would end eventually, and she needed to be somewhere safe when it did. Only there was no place left on Bellum Island that was safe for her.

It was only when they were stumbling slowly down the harbour road itself that Storm began to notice where they were heading. Scoundrel was taking her to the old warehouse cave where she had met the other witches. The monkey tugged, scolded, even beat at her with his tiny fists when she paused for too long. Once he threatened her with his sharp teeth, and she simply laughed wearily before staggering on.

They were lucky. No guards stumbled across them in the dark, and those people who did see them making their wavering, slow journey across the town must have assumed that she was just one of hundreds of drunken sailors travelling back to their night-time berths.

When Storm at last lifted deadened legs over the tumble of rubble at the mouth of the cave, she was too tired to do more than wince at the light that immediately flared.

"Thank the Ancestors!" The Earth-witch approached, carrying a lamp. "Are you hurt?"

"Just weary. Too much magic, I think. I need sleep."

"No time, I'm afraid. Your journey has only begun. You must leave Bellum tonight. It is too dangerous for you to stay longer."

"Journey where?" Storm blinked, shook her head

to try to clear it. "There's nowhere to go. The Fire-witch—"

"I know about the attack."

"How did you…" Storm sighed. She was obviously too tired even to think straight. "Did she survive? Do you know that?"

"I don't. The Tortoise told me of the attack and that you were battling for your life. I sent Scoundrel at once. The spirit said you would win."

"Huh." She shook her head, sudden tears burning her eyes. "It doesn't feel like it. A guard died! Perhaps others. It's my fault!"

"You haven't time for self-pity."

She glared at him.

"You didn't start the fight," said the old man, "and you are not responsible for those who are killed because the Salamander has no respect for life. The Fire Elemental is to blame, although I do not think the spirits understand such terms."

"Why do they have so much power without…"

"Without empathy? What we presume to call 'humanity'? One of the One's mysteries, I suppose. Although some say even the One did not create the Elementals. We must simply do our best, Storm. The Tortoise has spoken to me. You are to leave Bellum now, tonight."

"But what about the civil war? Talon?"

"Change is coming. My sources tell me that Waffa is opening secret negotiations with the leaders of the rebellion tomorrow. Doubtless she will challenge Talon for leadership. I think she will win. Hard as she is, she is no fool and knows that the Fifteen's days are numbered if they do not change. You have more work to do here, but now it is important that you survive. In order to do that, you must leave the island."

"How?"

"From this cave. The lava wall that protects the harbour is not this island's only mystery. Come, I will show you."

29

The Earth-witch took her arm and guided her deeper into the ancient warehouse. When they reached the rear of the cave, the yellow light of the lantern showed a jagged crack in the wall.

"Through there?" Storm hoped he would say no. The fissure must have been made by an earthquake and the idea of squeezing into the narrow opening was seriously unpleasant.

The Earth-witch nodded. "I will go first. Take care, the ground will be uneven."

He disappeared through the crack, taking the light with him. Storm sighed and squeezed through after the old man. Suddenly, she felt the oppressive weight of a mountain of clay and rock overhead. She was burrowing into the stone gut of Bellum Island.

It was too narrow to walk side by side so the old man led, lighting the way with his lantern. Storm paced behind him and last of all came Scoundrel, his tiny feet making soft pattering noises that were oddly comforting.

It was difficult going and they travelled slowly, crunching through rubble stone, pausing to climb waist-high blocks of rocks fallen from the ceiling of the crack. The walls of the fissure widened, grew moist, and then damp. The rocks they clambered over and around became treacherously slick with clay. Even the air she breathed changed: it tasted of deep, dark water. Of moss and slime. Of immense age.

So she was not surprised when they emerged from the crack in the earth on to a subterranean beach. Shingle crunched beneath her feet. Water lapped, restless, invisible, somewhere beyond the circle of lantern light. But it wasn't the sound of the underground sea that took Storm's breath away. It was what lay above them.

They had emerged into some sort of natural cavern. The reverberations of their footsteps made her think the cave was large although the ceiling hung only an arm-reach overhead. And it was alive with light! Storm stared up, mesmerised. Everywhere she looked she saw dots and chains of glowing blue-green lights.

"What are they?" she gasped.

"Glow-worms," said the Earth-witch. "Small creatures that live only here, far under the earth."

"It's beautiful." Her tiredness was forgotten for a moment. There was something truly magical about the carpet of glowing lights overhead. Like a constellation of blue-green stars that had never seen the sky.

"Yes. One of Bellum Island's most precious treasures, but one that cannot be traded or bartered. Come now. The boat is this way."

"Boat?" Storm stumbled after the Earth-witch, trying to look up at the glow-worms and walk at the same time. Scoundrel took her hand and pulled her after him with a wheeze of irritation. She had to smile: she would miss the creature's nagging. Her eyes grew hot. Where was she going? Wherever it was, it would be alone.

The ground began to slope downwards. The scent of ancient water increased, and at last Storm saw a pebbled shoreline and an expanse of black water that stretched out into the invisible distance. Its surface was as still as polished marble, and the reflections of the glow-worms shone in the water like drowned stars.

Green as the Snake Star – guiding star of all sailors. Storm's thoughts were stilled by wonder.

The lake lay before them, its surface unbroken by the slightest breath of wind. It seemed ensorcelled. A small canoe floated a few paces from shore, its mooring line tied to a large stone. The Earth-witch reached down, untied the line and drew the boat towards them. It glided soundlessly to shore, its wake carving ripples in the water.

He turned, handed the line to her. "This is your path, Storm. Let the Dolphin take you through the caves – it is a labyrinth, but the Water spirit will guide you. The boy will be waiting for you, when you come out from under the earth."

"Who?" She was exhausted; getting confused. The glow-worm light was hypnotic. She simply wanted to stare up at it and forget everything. "Who will be waiting?"

"The boy, Cloud. The glow-worm caves will take you to the outside. Outside Bellum Island itself. The labyrinth extends under the seabed to one of the small satellite islands outside the lava wall. The islands are too small for habitation. Only a few fisher-folk ever visit and never at night.

"The underwater river will take you there. It rises and

flows out of the earth into a small cove on the out-island. With the help of the other witches, I have arranged for Cloud to be waiting for you with a seaworthy canoe. Big enough for the two of you to leave this place and find your uncle's ship."

"You shouldn't have involved Cloud!"

"He seems eager to help. He said something about you not being the only one allowed to have adventures." He smiled at her, a kind smile of understanding. "And now, we say goodbye."

She bit her lip. "Thank you. I ... I will miss you. And Scoundrel." The words came out gruffly. Now that the time had come, she just wanted to be gone. She could not bear to look at the cling-monkey who was still holding tight to her hand. "Thank the others for me. Will I see you again?"

"When the time comes, you will find me. I am called Linnet. I came to Bellum several seasons ago to wait for you and prepare. Now I can return home. My island is on the edge of the world, but the right boat will find it, if the ship is sound and the sailor's heart true. Remember what I have said."

She nodded. "Goodbye, Linnet. Goodbye, Scoundrel."

"Scoundrel goes with you."

She stared at him, hardly daring to hope. "He can't. He loves you. Besides, it's too dangerous."

"The decision is not yours, Storm. Scoundrel has a job to do, as have you and I. See? He decides for himself!"

With a lash of his tail and a splash of black water, the cling-monkey bounded into the canoe and stood chattering impatiently at Storm.

"Off you go," said the Earth-witch. He laid a hand on her shoulder. "Travel with my blessing and love. Do your best, Storm, and all will be well. The Elementals have chosen wisely. Remember what I have said: do not depend upon magic. That is not why you were Chosen."

But magic was all she had to fight with. She bowed low, feeling unwise and far too young. Perhaps she would understand when she was less tired. Storm waded out into the water and climbed into the canoe.

She used a paddle to shove the boat off the gravel bank, then guided it out into the dark vastness of the cave-lake. A current caught at the hull, tugging, and Storm stowed the paddle.

Let the canoe drift where it would. Linnet had promised that the Dolphin would guide her safely through the maze of caverns. She sat, staring up at the countless lights of the glow-worms, Scoundrel a warmth leaning against her side. She hoped he wasn't missing Linnet too much, for there was no doubting the creature's love for his master.

Blue-green stars surrounded them, glowing overhead, reflected in the invisible depths of the water beneath her. Storm gave herself up to contemplation of their beauty, putting aside, for this brief time under earth, her fears and worries.

←——————→

She woke with a start, heart thudding, aware only that she was afraid, without knowing why.

Storm remembered: the old man; the glow-worm caves; Scoundrel. The boat still moved through the black water, but the glow-worms had disappeared. And the monkey's warmth was gone from her side.

"Scoundrel?" Darkness swallowed her voice, and Storm felt fear rise out of the unseen all around. A hiss came from the bow of the rowing boat – a "pay-attention!" grumble. Storm pushed herself upright. "What is it?"

Before the cling-monkey could admonish her again, she saw a circle of light, dim and faint, ahead in the darkness. They were at the end of the labyrinth! The Dolphin had delivered her to safety and freedom.

234

"Thank you, Water spirit!" she whispered. There was a quickening of the current. The boat sped forward. The circle of light expanded, pink and shining. Outside, under the sky, it must be dawn. The closer they got, the faster the water flowed, as the underwater river rushed towards the waiting sea.

Freedom! Soon she would see Cloud and her uncle, and be back aboard the *Wayfarer*! Bellum Island, with all its puzzles and challenges, would be far behind her and she would return home to Yanlin. Safe at home with Minnow! Safe for a season, at least.

Never before had she so looked forward to the monsoon season, when trading, and war, ceased. She would have half a year – much needed and precious time – to unravel the riddle of the Salamander's scheming and figure out her part in this war between the Elementals. She would have time to practise quiet magic. She would make another flute…

The mouth of light was upon them. Scoundrel bounded up and down in the prow of the canoe, chittering with delight as the little boat leapt from the darkness under earth into the morning of air and water.

And Fire.

Storm saw the line of people waiting for her. Two long war canoes were beached next to a small sea canoe. Slowly, she stood upright in her rowing boat, legs shaking with shock. With a shrill cry, Scoundrel launched himself at her. He climbed her body as though it was a sapling tree and hunched on her shoulders, long arms clinging tight around her neck. Expecting her to save him.

Cloud lay bound and gagged, tumbled on to the shingle of the beach. He was staring at her, angry frustration warring with fear in his eyes. Expecting her to save him.

The Fire-witch stood over him. Her long fingers danced in impatience. Storm barely gave the woman a glance. All her attention, both heart and mind, was focused on the person who waited for her – his eyes never leaving hers, his face as unreadable as ever. His people waded out, grabbed the bow rope and dragged her canoe to shore.

Storm stood, just managing to keep her balance as the boat was dragged high on to the shingled beach of the tree-shrouded cove. The Earth-witch had not betrayed her; she would not believe it. Someone had, but not Linnet. There would be time, perhaps, to find out, before…

Save them. Was it even possible? Perhaps she might be strong enough, lucky enough. She could only try.

But one thing she would accomplish, no matter what the cost! She would deal with *him*: the boy who had condemned her mother to death. Dain would be avenged!

Storm stepped out on to the shingled beach, the crying of seagulls in her ears, and walked forward to meet her enemy: Nim, the Drowned One.

30

When Nim was two paces away, Storm stopped walking. She gathered her magic as quietly and invisibly as hatred and shock allowed. Out of the corner of her eyes she saw the other Drowned Ones – more than a dozen of them, bows strung and at the ready, arrows notched and pointed. The Fire-witch was a column of red silk on the periphery. The strength of the woman's magic – and the force of her hatred – stank like ozone before a lightning storm. Scoundrel's arms tightened around Storm's neck, threatened to choke her. Cloud tried to shout something but only spluttered into his gag, his words strangled. Overhead, gulls screamed.

"Hello, Storm." Nim's eyes never left her face. He looks older, she thought.

"You've had your Choosing. That was the reward

your Elders gave you for betraying me."

He nodded.

"A Child of Fire?"

Nim shook his head. But he did not say which Elemental had Chosen him. Instead, he pointed to the witch guarding Cloud. "We found her in the sea where your whirlwind left her. She was half drowned. We saved her life."

"I never wanted her death."

"I believe you. But I doubt you're glad to see either of us alive. Especially me."

Storm drew breath, struggling to contain her emotions.

"The Fire-witch told us you would be here."

Something he had just said was important, but the idea slipped away, like a fish off a hook. She was shaking slightly with the strain of holding in her emotions, her magic. This was it. The moment she had planned, had dreamed of, since she held her dead mother in her arms. Retribution.

He didn't kill Dain! said her mind-voice. *Remember what the young Fire-witch said. The Salamander grows fat on hatred!*

"My mother is dead because of you." Her voice grated like stone. She stared at Nim, heart heavy with hate.

He nodded. His eyes brightened, as though with emotion.

Don't believe it! Such a liar. He had tricked her too many times. She couldn't trust him. Never again.

"I never wanted your mother's death," said the Drowned One boy. "I liked her. I am sorry. It isn't enough, I know, but I offer a life for a life." Nim gestured to where Cloud lay trussed like a parcel on the beach. "You come with us peacefully, and he goes free."

"Come with you?" She frowned, not understanding, studying his face for a clue. "Why?" And then realisation came, bringing sickness to the pit of her stomach. The Drowned Ones no longer wanted her dead. They wanted to own her, like the Pact, like Yanlin, like everyone. They wanted her magic for themselves.

Bile rose in her throat. A Drowned One's slave? Never!

No wings overshadowed them from the sky. No giant dolphin rose from the cove's waters. The Tortoise was silent. The Elementals were not here. Why? Always, in the past, when great danger had threatened, the spirits had appeared to her. Several times they had used their power to fight off the Salamander, saving her life. Now, when she faced her most hated enemy, they were absent.

The niggling thought returned: something Nim had just said was important. *She told us you would be here,* reminded her mind-voice.

"How did she know?" Storm asked him.

He frowned, puzzled, for a moment. Then realisation made him nod. "That you would be here?" He glanced at the Fire-witch, who smiled. Storm shuddered. The woman's smile was like the grin of a jackal, her teeth white, sharp and pointed.

The witch stepped forward, fingers twining, untwining, never still. "I found them! Your conspirators. The other witches." Her voice was melodic, beautiful. It made Storm blink with surprise.

"I knew of the traitor, the one who used to be a Fire-witch," continued the witch. "The Salamander told me about her treachery. I followed her, made her tell me everything. Then it was easy to track down the Air-witch, the Water-witch. I let them set the peasant boy on his journey here, thinking himself safe. Then I told the pirate clan, and we followed your shipmate's little boat. I came to meet you, Storm. You and I, we have a score to settle!"

"What did you do to them?" A chill was spreading from her heart. Her words puffed frost into the air.

"The traitress is dead: I owed that death to my

master. The other two? Perhaps they live. Perhaps not. If you meet them in the land of the Ancestors, then you will know." She smiled.

Linnet was safe at least. Scoundrel's arms were clinging tighter and tighter. She tugged at one, trying to loosen it, impatient. Why were the Elementals keeping away when the Fire-witch had attacked their Children?

The chill inside her grew. She still had her magic. Perhaps the Elementals knew she no longer needed their assistance. A moment before, she hadn't been sure, but Storm knew now that she could win this battle. The Drowned Ones had arrows and a Fire-witch. But she had her hatred.

Storm made herself think of Dain, let the knife of loss cut deep. Wind rose, bending the trees, scattering the top layer of shingle. The water of the cove began to churn. Sleet, like tiny darts, rained out the sky.

"Kill her!" screamed the Fire-witch. "She is too powerful – she will bring the ice! Shoot her!"

"No!" roared Nim. "You gave your word, Witch! If you attack Storm, I'll have you shot. We want her alive!"

Her enemy had just determined his own destruction! As Storm gathered her magic for the killing blow, she began to choke. Scoundrel had twisted around to cling to her chest. His arms were snaky vines around her neck, squeezing the breath from her. She tugged at a hairy arm, but the monkey was too strong – impossibly strong! Storm looked into the cling-monkey's eyes and saw, reflected in their brown irises, something ancient and unknowable yet instantly familiar. She flinched, but could not escape the gaze.

Scoundrel's mouth moved, and the Tortoise spoke: *You hold the Balance in your hand. The eternal war between fear and understanding, hatred and love, destruction and creation. Lose the Balance and hope dies.*

We Three took you as our child because you have the gift and curse of the story-teller: imagination. Because your parents loved and taught you well. But the choice is yours; it was always yours. Think of your mother's gifts, and choose!

The slow, gravelly voice faded from her head. Once more, Scoundrel was a tiny cling-monkey, shivering and crying plaintively. She cradled him to her chest.

Storm looked at Nim and thought of Dain. The answer was as warm and real as the monkey in her arms: Dain's talent had been for loving. For giving. For celebrating Life.

Storm hugged Scoundrel to her, needing his warmth. The wind died. The cove calmed. And when she spoke, her words no longer emerged on puffs of frost. "Cloud goes free. But I want to speak to him."

"Of course." Nim was breathing too fast, his face pale. But his eyes shone with relief and … gratitude? She must have imagined it.

Now that she had made her choice, the reality of what she had done made her feel nauseous. How could she bear to go with the pirates? To live as their slave? *Only for a little while*, soothed her mind-voice. *You will soon escape. Or something.*

Something, she thought, glancing at the Fire-witch. The woman returned her gaze with pure enmity. This one would not rest until Storm was dead. Did Nim really imagine he could control the Salamander?

A pirate untied Cloud, and Storm squatted beside him on the shingle. They talked in low voices, aware that the enemy was listening to everything.

"Don't try anything heroic, Cloud. Find Lake and the *Wayfarer*, tell them what has happened, and get back to Yanlin. I can look after myself."

"Why didn't you blast them?" He glared at her, furious, baffled … guilty. "Why did you back down? Why are you always such a coward? I didn't ask you to save me! Fight them. They are our mortal enemies – that's the only thing that matters! You can win. I know you can. Kill the Drowned Ones! For Thorn!"

She stared at him, her heart dry, and tried to find words he could understand. The look of betrayal in his eyes cut deep. He would never be able to forgive her for failing to be the sort of hero he believed in. She had not just lost a friend, she had made an enemy. Still she tried: "Sometimes, losing is how you win."

"Riddles!" He spat the word. "I thought you hated them."

"I do." She sighed. "Take Thorn's boat to Yanlin for me. Put it in his grave."

"You offer his spirit a toy instead of the vengeance he deserves." Contempt in his voice, his face.

Storm closed her eyes, feeling tired to the point of sickness. "Just take him the boat, please. Promise?"

"Yes." Sullen, but Cloud would take Thorn's boat to Yanlin.

In a few heartbeats, he was gone, bundled into the canoe and shoved out to sea. Storm watched the small red sail flick out of the cove and disappear behind a headland. When it had gone, she turned to face the Drowned Ones.

All her life, she had heard the stories her people told about the sea pirates. Had learned to tell them herself. Drowned Ones were not fully human. They lacked all virtue. Their islands had sunk beneath the sea because the people who lived on them deserved their ill luck.

The stories had taught her that the Drowned Ones were her enemy; that the only path for her people was that of war and vengeance. Against all that – the tales of her Ancestors' Ancestors' Ancestors, against the hate that still smouldered in her heart – she had only the words of the Tortoise and the memory of her mother. Storm saw the Fire-witch standing, waiting, fingers twitching, and wondered if it would be enough.

"I'm ready," she said.

Acknowledgements

Once again, a huge *Thank You!* to my amazing editor, Kirsty Stansfield, who nudged, guided and kept me on the right path throughout.

Thanks as well to the great team at Nosy Crow.

Continued appreciation goes to my agent, Jenny Savill of Andrew Nurnberg Associates.

My family and friends are old hands at writer-support now: I couldn't do it without you.